# THE BIG NOISE and Other Noises

## Christopher Kudyahakudadirwe

Mwanaka Media and Publishing Pvt Ltd,
Chitungwiza Zimbabwe
*
*Creativity, Wisdom and Beauty*

Publisher:

Mmap

Mwanaka Media and Publishing Pvt Ltd

24 Svosve Road, Zengeza 1

Chitungwiza Zimbabwe

mwanaka@yahoo.com

https//mwanakamediaandpublishing.weebly.com


Distributed in and outside N. America by African Books Collective

orders@africanbookscollective.com

www.africanbookscollective.com

ISBN: 978-1-77906-357-1

EAN: 9781779063571

DISCLAIMER
All views expressed in this publication are those of the author and do not necessarily reflect the views of Mmap.

# Dedication

This novel of short stories is dedicated, with all my love, to my wife Matha, who never believed I could write a book after a long time of aborted attempts.

# Chapter 1: When the Rabbit in a Grade 2 Textbook Moved

Two days before the 93-year-old president had announced his resignation through a letter written to the parliament of the country and army tanks had tracked into the capital city, I received a phone call which I did not expect. Looking at my phone's screen I saw Tonderai's name and number as it vibrated on the wooden table top. I could not believe my eyes. It had been a long time, almost three years if my calculations are correct, since I had communicated with my brother-in-law. Life is full of surprises. And questions too!

With hesitation and trepidation, I picked up the phone.

"*Tsano*, please."

"Impossible. I can't meet you. Not today. Like I've told you I've a deadline to meet. I've to submit this question paper by 8 o'clock tomorrow morning."

"Perhaps you will be happy if I'm dead."

That was it. I looked at the screen of the phone, now as if I was seeing Tonderai dying there. My mind was racing, collating and processing fragments of information all at once. Something must be really bad. The last time that I had talked to *Tsano* Tonderai was when he had bragged to me and two other men (my brothers-in-law) that he was not going to come begging for anything from us. That was on the day we buried his father, my father-in-law, and we had turned down his order to buy a cow to slaughter at the funeral. The economy was bad and money was not playing into our hands easily. The cost of living was galloping like a horse in a western movie after the rider has been shot down. It was then that he had categorically classified us as poor rabbits in a Grade 2 textbook. We only moved when the pages of the book were turned. Without an inkling of respect, Tonderai had thrown this to us in the presence of the mourners before throwing a bundle of money at our feet so we can go look for a cow to slaughter. This, among other invectives which are unprintable here, is what came into my mind as I looked at the phone.

"You're the only who can help me out of this." I heard his faint voice saying this from where I held the phone. I put the phone to my mouth and ear again.

"Where are you?"

"At Taguta Tavern near the kombi rank in town."

Responding to the urgency of his voice, I switched off my computer, put on a jacket and walked out of the house. I did call my wife to tell her where I was going, even if she was present she would not have allowed me to go. What her brother had said at the funeral had infuriated her so much that she did not consider him her brother anymore. She often told me that Tonderai treated us as if we were living with his sisters without paying *lobola* – like we were cohabiting.

The winter sun was painting the western horizon golden and a chill was settling in the air when I took a kombi to the city. The traffic was buzzing and zipping along the roads and streets of the capital city and the air was thick with its fumes. I took a seat next to the window where I could see the street lights as they popped on as night came upon the town like a washed black blanket being spread on a rock to dry. Questions without answers snaked through my mind as the kombi wove its way through the traffic honking and bumping along the much potholed road. Tonderai was a member of the secret service that had been serving the old president who had been put under house arrest two days ago. These were people who were very privileged in society and had access to the services that we, the ordinary citizens, did not have. I remember during the time when fuel was scarce, Tonderai would always be on the road in his Isuzu KB250 while the rest of the people had parked their *sikholokholos* due to the shortages of fuel. In fact, this was the reason why we, *vakuwasha*, had been classified as rabbits in a Grade 2 textbook. Being teachers, we earned very little so we could not afford a life of luxury during the economic meltdown that had engulfed the country. He was a BIG man; he had two houses; one in the high-density suburb and another in the low-density suburb to the north of the city which he was renting out to a Chinese family. I was renting two rooms in the satellite town 21 kilometres south of the city for my family.

Besides being a secret service operative, Tonderai also worked as an immigration officer at the country's borders which points to his other source of income and affluence. As was his nature, he often boasted that if he had no money to buy himself drinks he would follow any car with foreign registration number plates and stop the driver and then extort some cash from him or her. Thus, he always carried bundles of money with him all the time. During food shortages, when the country's dollar was as useful as toilet paper, there were always groceries in his house. Cross-border traders knew him very well. To be allowed to import more groceries and other goods into the country, they often paid him bribes in cash or kind.

But why did he want from me, a rabbit in a Grade 2 textbook which only moved when the pages were turned, then? One time I asked him to facilitate a passport for me from a neighbouring country and he flatly refused, accusing me of trying to put his job at risk but I had heard that he was doing it for so many other people for a steep fee. Perhaps he wanted me to pay for that service, I'm so sure now, but he never said that to me. If he had said I would have paid the bribe because that would have allowed me to go teach in that neighbouring country where teachers were being paid in US dollars. As far as I could see he wanted to help non-relatives than his relatives.

When I arrived at the tavern, I found Tonderai sitting at a table in the darkest corner, a cigarette with a long ash in his right hand and in his left a bottle of whisky that must have cost him a fortune. He was literally reading the ingredients of the whisky written on the label of the bottle, a sign that his head was swimming in the liquor.

"I'm here, *tsano*s." I announced my arrival as I pulled a chair to sit on the opposite side of the table. His face was like a tomato plant that had been uprooted and left in the October sun. Nervously he looked at me, the way an animal in the zoo behaves when a person approaches its cage.

He handed me the car keys without greeting me and stood up.

"I'll tell you everything in the car as you drive."

With a bit of hesitation Tonderai led me to his double-cab pick-up truck which was parked just outside the door of the tavern. Like a loyal dog, I followed him. Outside, the street lights were fully on and the traffic was punctuated by the voices of the *hwindis* - kombi touts - who were competing for passengers to come and board their kombis for their homes. A cold wind was blowing down the street picking up the used kombi tickets, wrappers of sweets, bits of newspapers, used recharge cards, that were strewn all over everywhere and carrying them the other side. From behind I could see that Tonderai was not steady on his feet.

"*Tsano*, let's drive away from here now. I've been too long in one place already." The words were slurred and came out the way a rhinoceros shat.

After familiarising with the dashboard of the truck, I switched on the engine and pulled away from the kerb. I pointed the car

7

towards where the wind was blowing from and drove carefully because there were too many kombis and knowing that their drivers had no respect for rules of the road, I did not want to dent my brother-in-law's truck unnecessarily.

"*Tsano*, I'm in trouble." He pushed in the cigarette lighter and lit himself a cigarette. I wound the window down. Since I stopped smoking fifteen years ago, tobacco smoke irritated me as if I had never smoked before.

"What trouble?" A sneeze sent cold shivers throughout my body.

"The soldiers want me." Mutilated words rolled out of his mouth.

"Why?"

"My friend who's a colonel in the army called me at 5pm telling me that if I wanted to save my life I had better leave the country right now."

I looked puzzled soliciting for further explanation. I did wait long.

"He said that all those secrete operatives who supported the beleaguered old president would be rounded up and executed the Chinese style and I'm one of those on the list. He said this would happen tomorrow after the march to the statehouse to protest the old president's reluctance to step down. So, *tsano* you're the only who can help me."

"How so?"

"I want you to drive me to the border so that I can skip the country tonight."

I slowed down and came to a halt by the side of the road. I looked at him in the eerie light entering the cabin of the truck. He looked at me and drew on his cigarette. The smoke from his lips filled the cabin as if a canister of teargas had been tossed into the

8

car. He sipped from his bottle before replacing it on the bottle holder on the dashboard.

"I don't think I can do that, *tsano*." I replied cockishly. "This is dangerous for me. What if we are stopped on the way, I'll be as much guilty as you are. They probably have your car number and will be on the lookout for those trying to skip the country. No, I'm sorry I can't help you." I made as if I was about to get out of the car.

"*Tsano*, if you don't want to help me, who do you think can help me and keep it a secret? I've sorted out the issue of the number plates. If they will be looking for this truck using number plates, they will not find it. I just want you to drive to the border post and drop me there and then you drive back in this very same truck. I've friends from the other country who will come and pick at the border. I've made arrangements already."

I was quiet for a while, thinking. This is the man who had refused to help me when things were not working well for me, I thought to myself. At the same time, he was the brother of my wife. It would be very cruel if I were to refuse to help him. The saying 'two wrongs do not make a right' kept creeping into my conscience at that time. At the same time, I was also agonising about what would happen if we were stopped by the soldiers on the way and Tonderai was found with me. Would they not accuse me of helping him to escape? Would I not be arrested together with him and punished just like him? I did not want to make my wife a widow yet and I still had a child in primary school.

"*Tsano*, here is some money for your trouble." He opened the glove compartment of the car and pulled out a bundle of notes and threw them on my lap. "You'll also keep this truck for yourself. My family doesn't need it anymore."

As we were parked there an army truck full of noisy and probably drunk soldiers drove past us. They were singing songs that were denigrating and at the same time urging the old president who was going through negotiations with the army generals at statehouse to step down. Whipped by this, I engaged gear and with a squeal of back wheels drove out of there to connect with the highway that would take us to the eastern border of the country. My mind was on the ward of money that was in the glove compartment and the prospects of having a strong vehicle like the one I was driving. The last car that I had owned was a 1983 Renault 5 that was as old as my first-born child. Now it was a broken shell parked at my rural home where the chickens were using it to lay their eggs as it waited to be cut up to make dishes out of its body metal.

We filled up at the next filling station along the highway. My brother-in-law said that we should not make frequent stop-overs on the way as these might increase our chances of being discovered and then everything would crumble. Around 8 I switched on the radio for the news. Yes, preparations for the following day's march had reached advanced stage. People had been advised to meet at the soccer stadium in the oldest location before marching to statehouse where they would show by sheer numbers that they wanted the old president to step down since he had presided over their problems for almost four decades. The minister and the youth leader who had been arrested had briefly appeared in court and were remanded in prison. The old president had been put under house arrest and a Catholic priest was helping with negotiations. An ex-president from the neighbouring country had arrived to persuade the old president to step down. In parliament they had started to go through the initial stages of an impeachment of the old president. The news was read by a military man and not by the usual news readers we knew.

From the capital city to the border town it was about three hours. We stopped in the last small town to fill up again and by 12:30am we saw the lights of the border town right below us. Tonderai, who had worked at the border town for more than five years before and knew the town so well, directed me through the town towards the border post which was just about five kilometres outside it. When we were seeing the lights of the border post, Tonderai asked me to stop by the road side. Without much ado he jumped from the passenger side and disappeared into the bush. I made a U-turn and drove back the way we had come.

Out of curiosity I checked the glove compartment. The ward of money was still there. I licked my lips.

When I drove into the eastern border town again, I looked for the main street and since it was around 3 in the morning I decided to park the truck and sleep. I could not drive back to the capital city. I was dog tired. When I found the best spot to park, I locked the doors of the car, wound up all the windows, collapsed the driver's seat backwards and reclined there on my back. Sleep did not waste time on a poor soul like me; in a short while I was snoring like a pig.

\*

The rising yellow sun was behind my back as I drove back to the capital city some 266 kilometres away. The road was littered by carcasses of small animals such as rabbits and snakes and nightjars that had been run over by vehicles during the night and crows were having a field day feasting on the carrion. As I gunned the *bakkie* along the road, I was wondering where Tonderai could be by that time but what really occupied my mind more was something else. This thing kept on leaping into my mind as much as I wanted to keep it out. Those who knew me knew that I did not have a car, let alone a powerful Isuzu KB250 that I was driving at that moment. Like I said before, my last car was broken down and was in the rural areas where the chickens had taken it over and were abusing it while awaiting the tinkers to skin the metal panels off and make buckets and pans out of it. How, then, was I going to explain to my neighbours this overnight acquisition of such a pick-up truck? To compound my problem, I did not have papers for the truck, that is if I was going to tell people that it was mine. Surely this would raise suspicions.

While that was the case, I was happy that there was a thick bundle of US$100 notes stashed in the glove compartment of the truck. That should be able to buy me a conscience to deal with the dilemma that I was immersed in at that moment. But it was good, it was good driving such a big vehicle. How I would be the talk of the whole community in which I stayed as well as where I taught? Would this not make my wife happy too? Think about it when I drove to my daughter's school to see her on a weekend, wouldn't she be proud that her dad had such a car? Another but? Yes! What about the soldiers who are looking for Tonderai? Would they be satisfied with the explanation that I would give if and when they approached me as one of the relatives looking for answers about his whereabouts? Well, … I told myself, I'll cross the bridge when I get there. I did not steal this vehicle and it doesn't carry Tonderai's number plate either.

As the distance between me and the capital city decreased and the winter midday clouds were hovering above covering the blue sky from me, I resolved to take the car to his wife in the suburbs where she stayed. I have no business owning such a vehicle, I told myself. After all teachers, who were the least loved by the government of the day, weren't earning much to have the luxury of driving such a vehicle. For the last four years or five we had been receiving our salaries in the middle of the next month. The government was broke and was living a hand-to- mouth-existence. Let me not go into deeper details of how the teachers had been turned into evil servants by the old president's government.

At 34 Cherrywood Avenue in the leafy northern suburb the gate was locked and a we-are-not-at-home-and-we-will-not-be-coming-back-soon atmosphere hung around the house like a cloud of teargas thrown to indignant vendors in the street. I tried Nelly's number but it immediately went to voicemail. I pressed the intercom – nothing! From the back of my mind I could hear what Tonderai had said: My family doesn't need it anymore. Immediately it dawned upon me that he had taken his family out of the country, too! With these words echoing at the back of my mind, I slowly climbed into the truck and drove to my house. Like I said before, my wife had visited her mother the previous week and I was only expecting her in two days' time. So, I was not a missing person at all. I took out the bundle of money from the glove compartment and went inside. As the yard at the house where I stayed was not designed for parking cars inside, I left the pick-up truck parked by the roadside.

In the house, in the privacy of my bedroom, on the comfort of my bed, I spread out the money to count it in order to assess my liquidity value. But as I was getting busy with that, I heard the sound of a car starting outside. I looked out through the window. The bakkie was screeching away from where I had parked it. I quickly ran out but it was too late for me to see who had taken the vehicle. Thoroughly defeated, I came back into the house and slumped on the bed on my back. I felt cheated? I considered my situation. Was it not a blessing in disguise that the truck had been stolen? How was I going to explain the car to my friends without raising suspicion? One thing that was certain though: I could not report the car as stolen because I was not the owner of the car; I did not have the papers for the car and neither had I memorised the registration number of the car. Of all the people who were related to me and even those not related to me, it was only Tonderai who knew what happened as from the previous day throughout the night and probably up to that day.

One hundred, two hundred, three hundred, four hundred: I was counting the money as I sat on the side of the bed. Unexpectedly, there was a knock on the door that interrupted my stock taking. On impulse, as if I had done this before many times, I picked a pillow and threw it on the money that was spread out on the bed. Through the keyhole where my outside view was restricted, I saw a blue shirt. The knock, ... again! Holding on to the door handle I cracked open the door. Violently, the knocker pushed the door wide and burst in.

"Where is the money?" Burning eyes bored holes into mine. I tried to avoid them as much as I could.

"What money?"

"Don't fucken waste my time! There was money in the car. Where's it?" The intruder drew a pistol from his jacket pocket. I heard a click from it. He used it to flick the pillow away from the bed and there was the money. Swiftly he scooped the money and stashed it in his pockets while keeping an eye on me. As soon as he was done he took out his phone, punched some numbers and spoke into it. In a short while Tonderai's pick-up truck came to a stop where I had parked it previously. The intruder snarled at me like a tiger, walked briskly to the *bakkie* and the doors banged and it drove off at high speed.

Subsequently I looked at myself and realised that like a rabbit in a Grade 2 textbook I had moved but remained on the same page.

# Chapter 2: A Long Story

Taneta opened her small imitation leather black handbag and fingered the small piece of paper inside. It felt smooth, crisp and reassuring. The girl had been checking on this piece of paper since she boarded the bus at Roadport in Harare. With it between her thumb and index finger she felt as confident as a baby whose father has tossed it into the air and would always catch it before it hitting the ground. The piece of paper was the only link between her and a new life she expected to start in Cape Town.

The Shosholoza Mail screeched to a final stop at Cape Town train station at exactly 15:17, the clock hung on the wall in the station announced it. The smell of steel wheels skidding on steel rails invaded the noses of the passengers crowded in the coaches. From the way all the passengers galvanised themselves into the action of getting off the train, Taneta could see that that was the end of her four-day journey. So, like the rest of the tired travellers, she removed her other bag from the luggage compartment and joined the stream of passengers disembarking on to the platform. She followed the people as they moved from the platform into the waiting space. As she emerged out of the platform, she asked the security guard standing by the exit where she could find public phones. She directed her. They were just outside the hall.

Taneta put down her bigger bag and searched for the small piece of paper in her hand bag. She inserted a R2 coin into the machine and picked up the handset. She punched in the ten digits that were written on the piece of paper and then placed the handset to her ear. She could hear dialling tones as connections were made wherever they were being made. In the space of waiting to hear the phone ring on the other side, Taneta's mind flew back to the time she was invited to come to this part of Africa. She met a distant cousin, who after seeing the state in which she was dressed and how thin she was, had invited her to come and join her in Cape Town so that she can look for a job and rid herself of the poverty that clung to her like a leech after warm blood. They met at the growth-point on Christmas Day. This was one of the few days in the year when young people in her village flocked to the growth-point like flying ants at the beginning of the rainy season. The girls and young women would be 'well dressed' in their multi-coloured clothes and tired hand-me-down high heels that leaned backwards or forwards like telephone poles after a severe thunderstorm. Their heads would be covered by Dolly Paton wigs that their mothers wore during their own courtship days. The boys would be resplendent in their second-hand jeans, sloppy Dynamos or CAPS United caps, faded T-shirts and smiling shoes.

It was Marita who saw her first.

"Daughter of my mother's sister's sister, how are you?" They were in the same grade at school.

"Not dead, sis!" Taneta was always like that. She never used the usual answers when asked how she was. "When did you come back from South?" She looked adoringly at Marita's Brazilian hair piece and pristine make-up. She only saw such make-up in old magazines that the lady teachers at her school used to buy when they had money to spare.

"Two days ago. I've been busy greeting everyone in my clan so I couldn't visit you."

"*Vasikana*, don't say that. Are you saying that I'm no longer part of your clan? Is it Cape Town that has changed you that much?"

"You know me, Taneta. I've always considered you as my real sister. If you think I don't mean my words, I want you to come and join me in Cape Town. The way you look, it appears you need a job and a bit of good care. Do you have a passport?"

The phone continued ringing until a woman's voice said: *The person you've called is not available. Please wait for the tone to leave a message.* Taneta cut the call. She looked at the number on the piece of paper again. Had she punched in all the numbers correctly? She redialled and after another short wait the same message came to her ear. This is the number that Marita gave me, she said to herself looking at it again and again. A cold snake slithered down her spine. Back at the village Marita had said she would be waiting for her at the train station as long as she scheduled to arrive on a Saturday or Sunday. And she had arrived on a Sunday as advised. She would have loved to come with Marita at the beginning of the year but then her passport was only going to be available at the end of February. That would have saved her all the anxiety that she was experiencing at that moment.

After what appeared to be a long wait, Taneta tried the number again, and once more the call could not go through. She thought she might not be making the call correctly. She was not used to telephones, so she went back to the security guard she had spoken to for help.

"You're not the only one, young lady," the elderly said as she threw the R2 rand coin into the coin slot and punched in the numbers on the piece of paper. "We have seen many people going through that. Those who would have invited them over choose not to come and fetch them and we normally have to direct them to the police for help."

"But Marita wouldn't do that to me. I'm …"

18

"Never mind how closely related you are to the person you're trying to call now. Wives and husbands have gone through this right here, sis *wam*." She listened to the handset and shook her head. "It seems your cousin sister's phone is off."

Taneta had never experienced fear of this nature before, not even when the ruling party people had come in the middle of the night to burn their home because they were suspected of being opposition party supporters, not even when she was in Grade 4 and had walked through the dark forest from her auntie and got lost for two days. All the stories she had heard about crime in South Africa crowded her mind fighting to come to the fore as if asking her to choose which she preferred. She had heard horrific stories of foreigners who had been laced with petrol and burnt alive, stories of defenceless people who had been stabbed to death for as little as R5, stories of women who had been gang raped by boys who had taken drugs, stories of children who had been trafficked and sold into prostitution and stories of people who had been killed and their body parts removed for *muti*. With all these stories playing in her mind, Taneta regretted having accepted the invitation to come to South Africa. At the back of her mind she cursed the day she had met Marita at the growth-point on that Christmas Day.

While she was struggling with her thoughts, trying to understand this difficult predicament she was in, some ChiShona words wafted to her ears from somewhere outside the train station hall. Quickly, she picked up her bag and rushed out so that she doesn't lose the chance to talk to people who spoke her language. Her hurry, as she discovered when she went outside, was unnecessary. Outside, she saw many people who spoke her language. They were packing their curio artefacts. Their day was over. Her ears felt good when, for the first time in three days, they heard a tongue she had grown up listening to. All along she had been wrestling with English and it had been a tedious experience for her.

The familiar home faces were so easy to relate to. All the five people she met there (three women and two men) were very friendly and it was like home coming for Taneta. There were many others who were there with their wooden and soapstone sculptures spread under the shade of the mutsamvi trees. They assured her of accommodation until she could get in touch with her cousin sister.

"The last time I called on this number is when I was at Park Station in Jo'burg and she had promised to come and wait for me here." Taneta said as she helped with closing shop.

"So many things could be the reason why she didn't turn up to meet you here. She will definitely have a good excuse for that," one of the men said.

The following day being a Sunday, the world woke up asleep. There were no cocks or birds like the drongo to wake people up in this part of the world. There was nowhere to hurry to – no fields to be weeded before it is too hot, no wells to rush to in order to fetch water before they are dry, no cattle to take out to the pastures before the dew is dry on the grass. On such a day, the day happened the way an egg is cracked from inside by a chick – slowly. Many had spent the last hours of Friday and the early hours of Saturday drinking in taverns and shebeens all over Gugulethu township.

Taneta was used to another regime of life that required one to wake up with the early birds and run life enhancing chores such as removing the previous day's ashes, making the fire, boiling water for people to wash their faces and sweeping the yard. So, on this day despite being very tired after the long journey from Harare, Taneta woke up with the sun when everyone else was asleep. Her mother had always insisted that a woman must always wake up early and make sure the home is in order before visitors start arriving. Since it was summer, the day started a little after half-past 5. If Taneta had not been new at this place, she would have started by sweeping the yard, after which she would wash last night's dishes and then later make breakfast - in that order. But being newly arrived, she lay in the crude bed she had been assigned to wait for those who were the owners of the place to give her directions on what to do.

This lying-in was a recipe for deep reflection. The young woman's mind went back many miles to her rural village in Rushinga District. It arrived there to see what was happening at that time of the day. First, she trained her mind on what her mother would be doing at that hour. Of course, it being a Sunday she would already have gone to the borehole to fetch water which she would boil to bath her grandchild, the child of Taneta's elder sister, so they can go to church together. After that she would iron her Salvation Army uniform and carefully starch the hat. She would feed the poor child left over sadza and okra and then they would troop to church – the grandson leading carrying her *gogo*'s tambourine and not the old warn-out Bible. Taneta knew this because it was her mother's Sunday routine and if she had been there she would walk with her while the frolicking child led the way a few metres ahead.

One of the women who had slept at the other end of shack stirred. By now shafts of sunlight were coming through the many holes in the walls of the shack at an angle of more than forty-five degrees. The shacks had been built using used corrugated iron sheets. It was through the holes made by the first nails when the sheets were still virgin that the sunlight was coming through. It was going to be a hot day.

"*Ndeipi?*" She greeted Taneta in ChiShona while running an open palm down her face briefly covering the long yawn from her mouth. This was the one called Shingi whom she later knew was called Shingirirai in full.

"It would seem that today isn't a day to you people." Taneta pushed away the blanket covering her lower body. She stood up and stretched raising her hands up such that they reached the roof of the shack.

"Sure, sis. Sunday doesn't bring us any money but we need to eat on a day like this. You shall see that foreigners who are in this country came to make money. They have no time for other things." She stretched and yawned again. "Were you working back home?"

"I've never worked all my life unless if you mean working in my mother's field. If ever I'm going to work it will be here."

"Why do you think your cousin sister blocked your call? Was she really your relative or it's the bus stop kind of relationship?"

"She is, but a little distant. She is a daughter of the sister of my mother's co-wife. She promised me that she would have a job ready for me when I arrive." Taneta spoke like a congregant of one those churches where people are promised more if they give all they have as tithes.

"You need to try the number again in the afternoon. Maybe she couldn't take the call at the time. Some of the white people that some of us work for do not allow people to take calls in their houses." Shingi stood up from the mattress she was sharing with the other woman whose name Taneta still had to know.

After she had used the blue plastic mobile toilet buzzing with green bombers at the edge of the yard, she showed Taneta how to bath in their shack. After that they had a cup of black tea each. Then Shingi asked Taneta to accompany her to the hairdresser. As a curio merchant, she wanted to enhance her dreadlocks so as to sync with her business demands. It was generally believed that people who dealt in stone and wood sculptors presented themselves better if they wore dreadlocks. The other lady, whom Taneta came to know later as Shirley, remained behind doing her washing.

*

The hairdresser's shop, together with various other small shops, was near the train station at Nyanga Junction. It was run by a Zimbabwean lady and her two Zimbabwean assistants. They plaited, twisted, shampooed, curled, shaved, sewed on weaves, braided, relaxed and tinted people's hair. They also had a department for men's haircuts as well as beard grooming. The place also acted as a shop for food stuffs from Zimbabwe. On the shelves one could go home with *mufushwa, Kapenta matemba, madora* and dried *derere*. They even had distilled *hundi* in stock for the *derere*. It was also a meeting place for homesick Zimbabweans as well as a postal agent for letters and money going to and coming from Zimbabwe. When time allowed, like on Sundays and Saturday afternoons, Zimbabwean people gathered there to exchange news and views about the political situation back in their country. It was a place where people discussed how to get papers from Home Affairs, how to look for jobs and how to avoid being robbed by the notorious skollies of the townships.

By 11 o'clock the air surrounding the tuckshops was grey with the smoke of braai fires as well as the steam from the sizzling fleshes of beef, mutton, chicken and fish. A blend of scorched smells of these wafted through the door of the salon reminding Taneta of those rare days when a goat was slaughtered back home and there was a lot of meat to roast and cook and eat. Beautiful cars were parked by the road side, their doors and boots open and house music was booming out of them. From the salon, the music was one loud blaring sound that was punctuated by bass drums that kept the time differently depending on when the discs started playing.

Men and women sat in the cars or on bonnets or on canvas beach chairs strangling quarts of beer by their necks, clutching glasses of gin or whisky in their hands and balancing platters of freshly roasted meat on their knees. Taneta had never seen such indulgence in her life. Dogs mingled with the carousing people picking up the bones that the revellers threw away. Some couples walked up and down, their free hands encircling each other's waist. Sometimes they would stop and kiss and Taneta looked away when they kissed. She felt like she was spying on them. This was Mzansi, she was to know later.

The salon was like an employment exchange too. Everyday Zimbabweans passed by leaving messages of job vacancies that will have arisen where people worked and needed filling up. They also left behind tales of what would have happened at the building sites, the kitchens, the gardens and the Chinese shops where they worked. They would report about where people had been fired and the employers needed replacements. Taneta learnt that Tuesdays and Wednesdays were the days that provided good opportunities for one to land a job. Local people had become known for being lazy by the employers. It was common that they did not report for duty the following Monday after pay day. So, employers preferred foreigners, especially Zimbabweans and Malawians who had become known for their loyalty and hard work. It was also known that they accepted lower wages too. This made them enemies of the South Africans who just wanted jobs but they did not want to work.

"Do you have asylum, sis?" A woman whose head was inside a dryer asked Taneta.

"What is asylum?" There were a lot of words that Taneta had to learn quickly.

"It is a paper, like an ID, that you get from Home Affairs in Nyanga. It makes you legal to be here in Mzansi."

"I only arrived yesterday, *mufunge*. This is my first day in Cape Town."

"If you had that paper you would have come with me tomorrow. A white family next to where I work in Claremont requires a maid as soon as yesterday."

"Oh, is that so?" Taneta was left wondering. "How can I get that asylum then?"

"You must go to Home Affairs for that as soon as possible." Shingi said. It was good that she did not tell the people in the salon that Taneta's cousin sister who had invited her to Cape Town had not responded to her attempts to communicate with Taneta. She did not even say she was accommodating her temporarily while she sorted out her life.

The February sun was setting Gugulethu on fire by the time Shingi's dreadlocks had been washed, dried and re-twisted to deal with the growth. Rumbles of hunger were rocking Taneta's stomach as if there was a thunderstorm brewing inside it. She was not used to the eating regime of these people, but since she was not in her mother's house she wouldn't do as she pleased when it came to cooking and eating. But the trip to the hairdresser's shop had furnished her with a lot of knowledge as to how to start life in Cape Town.

Monday morning, as early as the time that she would have woken up to go and await her turn to fetch water at the village well, Taneta was squeezed between two men in a queue at Nyanga

25

Refugee Reception Centre. She had never been that close to a man as to feel the man's manhood pressed hard on her bums. By the time the sun peeped above the eastern horizon her legs were aching and the queue was snaking its way for over three hundred metres along the walls of the factories nearby. There were those who wanted to renew their asylum papers, those applying for the first time like Taneta, those seeking permanent residence, those seeking refugee status and those who were doing family joining. There were people from Zimbabwe, Zambia, Togo, Nigeria, DRC, Mozambique, Kenya, China, Pakistan and Malawi. The place could have been the Tower of Babel judging by the diversity of languages she heard being spoken around her.

Those who spoke the same language, if they happen to be close to each other, were telling each other how they had come to be in Cape Town. Some Zimbabweans just three people ahead of her were telling each how they had crossed the flooded Limpopo River when one of them was snatched by a crocodile. There were stories of how some of the people there had been accosted by skollies, fought them off or were robbed of their cheap phones. Taneta also heard stories of how some people bribed the security guards so that they could be allowed entrance in the offices ahead of the rest of the refugees. She was absorbing all this education quietly like a school child who had joined a new class in another school.

When the offices opened at eight, there was much pushing and pulling for position. Taneta had to put her arms around the man in front of her so that she does not lose her place. All dignity and morality had to be hung on the nail of conscience in such a situation, she realised. She suspected that a lot of pickpocketing could be taking place during such a melee so she held on to the money and the small phone that she had been lent by Shingi with vice-grip fingers. All this made Taneta regret her going away from the comfort of Rushinga.

People were admitted in batches of sixty at a time and she was lucky to be number fifty-four. Three hours later she emerged from the office brandishing an asylum seeker application document valid for nine months. She could look for work, she could study and she could open a bank account, so the paper said when she read it later at home.

*

There were many 'firing points' in Cape Town. 'Firing points' were places, usually by the roadside, where job-seeking people waited in the morning and those looking for casual workers visited to hire people on a temporary basis. There was one behind Nyanga Junction which was for the construction workers. The one for house maids was in Green Point, so Taneta had to wake up early, catch a train into the CBD and then walk to that 'firing point'. Shingirirai had given her directions the previous night. When she arrived there, she stood amongst the others and had to learn how to solicit for hire. The women would raise their forefingers to signal that they were available for hire. As soon as a car stopped, the ladies would swarm around the window hoping to be chosen. Taneta stood aloof as the first cars came and some women were picked for work. At about nine o'clock, a big Audi Q7 came to a halt at the 'firing point'. The rest of the women went to the window of the white lady's car but the lady did not choose them.

"I want the one who is standing there," the white woman shouted above the chattering women. She was pointing at Taneta.

Taneta looked behind her thinking the lady meant someone behind her. "You mean, me!" She pointed at her chest.

The white lady nodded her greying head. "Yes, you! Come, get in!"

Taneta went to the other side of the big car and climbed in. Her hearing was temporarily impaired by her thudding heart. She had not expected to get a job so easily. Maybe the white lady is not serious, she told herself as the car screeched up towards Kloof Nek and then down to Camps Bay. A lot of questions swamped her mind: will I be able to cope with all the household equipment that I have heard white people use in their houses? My English isn't up to scratch, will I be able to speak well? What about setting the table? All these disturbing questions wormed through Taneta's mind. Her heart was thumping in her chest like the funeral drum they played back home when someone died.

"Have you worked in a house before?"

Taneta wanted to say: yes, but she did not want to create a situation where when they got to the house she would be assigned work that she did not know how to carry out. Taneta shook her head the way a newly born calf does on the first day it is introduced to the dip tank.

"No, madam." She did not even know to what question she had answered with that 'no, madam'. She looked ahead fearing that the lady was going to stop and tell her to get down so she could go back and get someone who had experience before she had gone far from the 'firing point'.

"Good. You're the kind of person I'm looking for. People who have experience are difficult to train according to my standards."

Taneta looked at her with surprise in her eyes.

"I'm Liz. What's yours?"

"Taneta." She looked around the car. It had a very pleasant smell that made her feel dirty. She could pick the smell of the shack in which she had slept for three nights.

"You should be from Zimbabwe, I guess. Your accent says it."

"Yes, madam."

"I saw you there and thought so. That's why I chose you."

\*

It was not very difficult to learn how to work in the house, Taneta realised after a week of going through her orientation. She was a quick learner. Soon she was working on her own. She dusted, cleaned, washed, ironed, polished, vacuum cleaned, but she did not cook. The lady cooked for her family when they did not go to eat out. She was given a room at the back with a toilet and bathroom, DSTV and a small kitchen. She went back to Gugulethu the following weekend to fetch her bag of extra clothes.

One sunny mid-morning Taneta was putting the washing on the line when she happened to raise her eyes and saw another black woman walking back into the house next door. The woman was wearing a maid's uniform. She did not see her face, but something about the way the woman walked rang a distant bell in her mind. Taneta told herself that people were similar in many ways though. With time, Taneta became very curious, not because she wanted to know who that woman was, but because she wanted another black face with whom she could identify with, maybe someone of her level and disposition with whom she could talk to. So, she kept looking out for a chance to see her again.

The following Monday Taneta wheeled the first rubbish bin to the gate where the dumpsters would come and pick them later that morning. She went in to fetch the second one. When she came out with the second one, the maid from next door was also coming out with a bin from there.

"Hello, there." Taneta did not want to lose this chance that had arisen.

The other woman was not facing her, but when she turned around to acknowledge the greeting, Taneta's heart skipped a bit. Was this not Marita her cousin sister? She dumped the bin and rushed to her. They hugged and cooed and kissed each other's cheeks. Tears of joy rolled down their eyes before they held each other apart and examined each other for a little while.

"Daughter of my mother's sister's sister, how are you?"

"I'm fine dearest. When did you arrive here?"

"A week ago. I've been trying to call you but could not get through."

"Oh, Taneta. It's a long story. When you called me while you were in Joburg, I was going to Khayelitsha by train. When I answered your call some skollies saw me answering your call. As soon as I finished speaking they asked me to give them my phone or they would stab me if I refused. So, I don't have a phone right now. I'm sorry for the trouble that it must have caused you."

"Not much though I was afraid that something worse was going to happen to me. I was helped by some people from home at the station. They stay in Gugulethu. That's where I was staying until I got this job. I'm so happy to see you and to be working on the same street with you. We must thank God that we are together as we had arranged in the first place. Let's meet again at lunch time and talk."

"Sure, sis. My lunch is at one."

"So is mine."

# Chapter 3: Between a Rock and a Hard Place

*B*umharutsva, the first heavy rains of the beginning of the rainy season, had come and gone a day ago. The black soot from burnt forests and vleis had been swept away and in its place, green shoots of succulent grass, much loved by cattle at the beginning of the rainy season, were sprouting. It was also that time when cattle can get lost never to be found as they are deceived by the greenery of the shooting grass – the grass is greener on the other side mantra! Looking a hundred metres ahead of it, a cow would see the green ahead and think there is a lot there, but when it gets there it will find the greener pastures still ahead. When the cow lifts its head, and looks ahead, it will again think that the grass greener is ahead and this makes it keep going until it is lost. For our people, it is time to start ploughing their fields preparing to bury the seed for next year's harvest.

Karasa arrived home lugging a twenty-five-kilogram bag of seed maize that his family was going to sow the following day. He had been to the growth-point where he bought the bag. He was a little drunk after having used the change from the ten dollars he had taken with him to buy the seed maize to buy a *zangata* of opaque beer. His wife rekindled the fire which was almost dead to warm his supper.

"Baba vaMucha, the children told me that Harare is not in the kraal with Chikurubi." Karasa's wife blew on the two logs in the fireplace. The logs sparked like fireworks at a New Year's Day celebrations, maybe a snake had slithered over them while they were still in the bush, so our myth said. A flame came to life.

"It can't be far. Have they been to the dam looking for it? That's where I found them last time when they did not come back." Some spittle jumped out of his mouth as he spoke. He continued to gnaw the drumstick with his canines since he had no front teeth.

"*Ehe*, I sent them there but they did not find it. Tomorrow morning, they are not going to school. They must look for it at all the nearby village kraals. Time to plough is running out. We need to finish that portion by the anthill and throw the seed in the ground as soon as possible."

"Yes, you're right, *mai mwana*. We need to be in the race with the others. I'm sure Witbooi is not very far. Since we started giving them salt every evening they have never strayed far. They have often been here before sunset." Karasa washed his hands in the dish that his wife held before him. He dried his hands on the sides of the coat he was wearing.

"Tomorrow you must also wake up with the roosters and look for it. If we don't sow this week we may not gather a good harvest this season. You know the rains of these years are tricky." She packed the dishes away and started making *mahewu* for Karasa and the children. They will carry that when they go looking for the lost ox the following day.

Karasa sat back on the earthen bench in the round hut. From his back pocket he took out his tobacco pouch. In it was a piece of newspaper and some tobacco. He rolled a cigarette and lit it with an ember he pulled out of the fireplace. Soon the hut was choking with tobacco smoke. "Yes, tomorrow I will wake up and go looking for this stupid ox which seem to have forgotten where home is." He said this in between chest rending coughs.

"Maybe it is afraid of the yoke. It's been a long time since they were yoked. They have forgotten what a yoke is."

32

"Maybe." He coughed again. The tobacco stung his lungs.

The following morning Karasa beat the roosters at their crowing game. By the time the sun peeped on the land from behind the eastern mountains, he was four villages away from home. He had followed all the cattle kraals in all those villages checking but Harare was not there. When the villagers started to walk about as they prepared to go to their fields, he inquired about a giant black ox with a white spot on its forehead and down-turned horns.

"It was with the chief's herd yesterday," the first person he met pointed to a homestead perched on the brow of a hill. "Maybe it could still be there."

After thanking the man, Karasa raced towards the chief's home. But Harare was not there. He asked the chief's child who was at the kraal milking the cows. What he was told was not encouraging. By this time the summer sun was making the trees and the huts dance in its heat; perhaps they danced to the cicadas' songs which came from the newly leafed trees where they were perched. Karasa remembered his *chigubhu* of *mahewu*. He sat by the bank of the dust road to take a swig or two. He made himself the first cigarette of the day and tried to puff away his frustration. In the fields and on both sides of the road, Karasa could see spans of oxen going up and down and behind them the ploughs tearing the earth brown. The smell of freshly turned soil wafted to his nostrils with a familiarity that made him realise that he was behind time in the race of preparing the fields. The crack of whips on the backs of the yoked animals, the whistles of the drivers as they urged the spans and the sound of the wheels of the ploughs came to him from all sides. Humid mid-morning air breezed over his body where his skin was bare. A thunder shower could be brewing for the afternoon.

Karasa crushed his cigarette on a stone beside him. He trudged through the villages, up the hills and down the other side, across rivers that flowed with the murky waters of early summer. The people he asked about Harare directed him to the east, to the west, to the north – to all directions. They said that they had seen the ox there with this or that herd. It was a long day.

By the time the sun was about to hide behind the western mountains, Karasa was very far away from home. The stories he was told by the people he asked about Harare were that they had seen it that morning and that he would find it before the day ended. To him that was like running after the 'water' on a tarred road on a hot October afternoon.

The sun winked farewell to the world and darkness started to clothe the world around Karasa. He started to think of where he was going to sleep. Home was very far away now. The search for Harare could only be resumed the following day. As he walked through the leafy green forest he heard the thump-thump of a cowhide drum. His instinct told him that there was a beer party where that drum was being thumped. He force-marched himself towards the homestead. From a distance and in the twilight, he could see that this was a big home that stretched almost half a mile. The number of huts which had palls of smoke rising from their conical roofs told him that the place belonged to a man who had five wives. A drunken gathering of men and women was at the far end of the homestead where they were singing and dancing to the accompaniment of the cowhide drum. They were also drinking and eating chunks of meat that was roasting on an open fire.

After a long day of trekking through the open fields and the greening forests there was nothing so welcome as a *zangata* of *rapoko* beer and a piece of juicy meat. Soon Karasa had lost himself in the revelry of the villagers. He knew no one and no one knew him. He ate and drank and danced and smoked. As time went by he forgot why he had come that far. He even forgot that he had a wife

34

and children who were waiting for him to come back with Harare to plough the fields so they could sow their crops. He forgot that he was looking for a lost beast and that the following day he was going to resume the search. He whirled round and round with the women dancers whom he joined in the arena. He stamped his feet and shook his backside with them. He lost track of time. He even forgot his name …

The third cry of the roosters invaded his mind from far away. He must have been dreaming. Semi-consciously he explored where he lay. His fingers touched a naked body snoring beside him; a breast. There was a woman beside him on the bed. At first, he thought it was his wife but there was something strange about everything. This was not his bedroom. When he put his arm around the woman's waist, he discovered she was thinner than his wife. The positions of the windows of the room were also not the same as what was familiar to him. Some recollection of what might have happened started to seep into his mind. He quickly sat up on the bed. The morning light that was filtering through the curtained window was not enough for him to make much of the room. He shook the woman. She murmured something he failed to understand. She sidled over and put her arms around him.

"Hey, where am I?" His voice sounded strange in his own ears. He wriggled out of the woman's arms.

"Come back to bed. Hold me in your arms. I'm all yours. I'm starved in this place." She tried to force him to lie on the bed.

"No! Who are you?" Karasa was now looking for his clothes. His hand brushed against a box of matches. He picked up the box and struck one stick. He looked for the lamp. He knew it could only be by the bedside. He saw it standing on a small table. He lit it. The yellow light revealed that the woman who was lying on the bed was one of the wives of the man of the homestead. He had heard the other women he had danced with talking about her the previous night.

Karasa jumped to his feet. He put on his trousers quickly. He knew he was in trouble if he was found in that room. He looked for his shoes. They were not where he thought they were. He bumped his head on the bedpost. He saw stars in the darkness of the room. His head was spinning. He picked the lamp; went on his knees. He peered under the bed. What he saw shocked him. Karasa came face to face with the face of Harare, his lost ox. Harare's glassy eyes fixed him with an unblinking and lifeless gaze. The frozen gaze transfixed him in that kneeling position for a while. It was as if the animal was saying here I am, take me home. Death was not registered on the face of the ox.

The man quickly groped for his shirt and ran out of the house with it in his hand. He took the direction he had approached the home from and ran until he arrived at a ford on the river he had crossed the previous day. He sat on a rock and started to think.

"Where am I running to, leaving my ox there? I must report these people for slaughtering one of my oxen. But how will I explain how I have discovered the head of Harare? The husband of that woman will definitely sue me for adultery. My family is ruined now. How am I going to plough my fields with one ox? How am I going to tell my wife that Harare has been slaughtered at the home that I have just fled?" He said all this and much more. In his mind he kept on seeing the face of Harare – the spot on its forehead and the turned-down horns.

Those who saw him sitting on the rock talking to himself pointing this way and that way thought he was a mad man.

# Chapter 4: Garden of Agony

I'm lying on an old hessian sack that smells of goat urine and manure. The smell of goats has always been unwelcomed to my nostrils, but who cares tonight? The luxury of cosy blankets and soft pillows is not for me tonight as it was many nights ago. The starry sky is my blanket and the hard earth my bed. My bedroom is a garden, which has a thick banana plantation on one side and a small patch of vegetables – some rape, a few cabbage heads and legumes of doubtful hybridity – on the other. A slow-flowing perennial stream snakes its way through the garden, dividing it into two. The bananas and vegetables are growing on its banks.

The dark September sky is punctured by sparkling stars. The stars remind me of a story I heard when I was still very young, telling that those stars are small holes in the floor of heaven and reveal its brilliance. The Milky Way is running askew across this sky. It would be such a beautiful night if all things were equal, but the desire to admire such a scene is far from my instincts now. Not tonight, when far-distant mortar explosions and the crack of gun-fires are floating to me through the dense night air reminding me that a war is raging all-round the country. No, not tonight when I know lurking somewhere is a posse of soldiers hunting for me.

From the dug-up and watered patch of the garden the damp smell of riverine soil mixes with the smell of the goat urine and manure and causes me to suppress a great urge to sneeze. Sneezing is the last thing that I would like to enjoy at this moment. This smell has been in my nose ever since I jumped into this garden seeking cover for the night. The soldiers followed my tracks throughout the afternoon until I managed to cheat their vigilance by jumping into a pool and concealing myself under the water. I spent the better part of the afternoon under-water with only my nose protruding to catch some air. The pool was on the lower part of the same stream that runs through the garden where I lay but here there were many trees on the banks.

Mosquitoes whine as they fly past my ears in their ecstatic search for my exposed arms, face and ankles. I'm sure most of them haven't tasted human blood during their short life. They fall over each other, scrambling for space to land and dip their needles to suck me up. The temptation to squash them with my open palms is so great, but I can't. I'm afraid of making that clapping noise that might reveal my hiding place to the soldiers. I have to squeeze their tiny bodies against mine to kill them. They have already perforated my exposed skin, creating bumps that are so sore and requiring frequent scratching.

At this point my mind slips into the past, bringing the events of the previous day into focus. We were seated under the shed of my father's bedroom hut, playing cards to kill the long hours of the chimurenga war days. The three of us: my friend who liked to call himself A1, my older brother and I, liked to sit here where we could see far and wide. Our homestead's position on a knoll enabled us to see the soldiers when they were still far away affording us time to run into the thick bushes to the west of the village to hide.

Most often we would be listening to a two-band short-wave radio that my father had bought for us when he returned from a two-year political detention at Gonakudzingwa. Our favourite radio station was LM Radio which broadcasted from Lourenço Marques in Mozambique. We liked this radio station because it played pop music – the kind that we enjoyed at boarding school during those days. The small radio sometimes alerted us when soldiers were approaching. When the soldiers were in the area and using their walkie-talkies, it whizzed and shrilled, the frequencies colliding. Sometimes we even picked up their voices clearly and we would listen to snatches of their messages. But on this day, the battery was flat and we relied on our eyes and ears.

It was the sound of motorbikes that alerted A1 to the approach of the soldiers and he pointed in their direction. They were rushing across the brown fields towards us with dust billowing behind them like those airplanes that spew smoke in flight. We had recently heard that they were now using bikes to chase and shoot village boys and girls whom they thought were helping the freedom fighters. The village boys were called *mujibhas* and the girls were *chimbwidos*. We were the *mujibhas*. So, we took flight towards the bush with G3 and FN bullets whizzing in the air around us. I could see small branches of trees falling from trees where they had been nipped by the whizzing bullets. As soon as we reached the edge of the bushes, we split up, each one in his direction. The freedom fighters, also known as 'boys', had taught us some basic survival tactics. I ran towards this small river and jumped into a deep pool which was overgrown by trees such that the tree branches almost over-hung right to the middle of the pool. When the sun sank and darkness enveloped the country-side, I came out of the water, drenched, my body whitish all over from being too long under the water. I plodded upstream, looking for a place to spend the night.

The night goes by slowly. The Milky Way shifts like the hand of a giant clock whose dial is the star-spangled night sky. From previous observations, I know that when the starry band is running east to west, the day will be breaking soon, but I cannot tell the exact time. The cocks in our village are good at keeping time for us, but there are no cocks or hens left. They have been slaughtered for the freedom fighters who always like to eat *sadza* with chicken and nothing else. If dogs could take over their duty, it would be very welcome tonight because they are abundant and their barking carries far, but dogs have never been good at keeping time.

Eventually the eastern horizon begins to redden. Twilight heralds the rising of the big star and the beginning of another day of cat-and-mouse brushes with the Rhodesian soldiers. The strengthening light chases the mosquitoes to the darker corners of the plantation to my great relief. Their feeding is over for the day.

One of the poles from the garden gate squeaks and tells me that there is someone coming into my hiding place. Instinctively, I quickly roll behind a bed of cabbage heads as my heart jumps into my mouth. Have the Rhodesian forces woken up so early to flush me out? Perhaps they saw me from afar with their binoculars and have come to fetch me. To my relief, it is the owner of the garden coming to work. I stand up, my knees weak with fright and we greet each other. He asks why I'm in his garden that early. I know him. He knows me, too. But I can see that he is suspicious of my presence there. Perhaps he thinks I'm there to steal his vegetables. I tell him that I had to spend the night in his garden hiding from government soldiers. He understands. He sympathises with me. The soldiers are after the *mujibhas* and the *chimbwidos* who are the messengers of the 'boys' and not elderly people like him. He knows this, too. Capturing a *mujibha* or a *chimbwido* and torturing him or her provided them with valuable information about the whereabouts of the terrorists and the kind of arms that they would be carrying. This man knows what is happening around the country.

By now the rays of the September sun are becoming needles. They are already attacking our bare skin demanding that we seek the relief of some shade. The green vegetables are already bowing down to them. While the gardener and I are busy talking an authoritative voice challenges us. I dive into the leafy green of the banana trees and crawl deep into the mulch of the cast-off brown leaves.

'Don't waste your time hiding! We've already seen you, terrorist! Just come out before we shoot you!'

This is the beginning of my agony.

# Chapter 5: Loving Beyond Boundaries

When the shopkeeper handed Nyaradzai the letter, she immediately knew it was from Nyaradzo, her twin-sister, who was at school in the big city. Nyaradzai knew her sister's handwriting the way she knew 'their face' every time she looked in the mirror. Their likeness was shared in almost every aspect of their lives – looks, temperaments, gaiety, speaking, blinking – many people always failed to tell the difference between the two girls. It was even rumoured in the village that they had shared one boyfriend when they were in primary school. But at this point in their lives they had been separated. Eight months ago, Nyaradzai had left school and eloped to the east of the country after she fell pregnant. Their mother had then asked her brother, Chake, to come and fetch Nyaradzo so that she may finish school in the big city under his strict eye. And that ended their co-existence in the dusty village to the north of the country. Besides the occasional phone calls and SMSes they exchanged, there had been no other form of communication that could stitch them back together again. This fat letter was a big surprise to Nyaradzai especially when many people had stopped writing letters many, many years ago.

The letter was in a khaki A5 envelope and the postal stamp confirmed where it originated from. Nyaradzai turned the envelope around, there was nothing written at the back. She thought of opening it there and then but she hesitated before carefully folding it and tucking it away in her luxurious chest. Her pregnancy had reached an advanced stage and she had come to the growth-point clinic for the scheduled pre-natal check-up. So, when she had finished her check-up she went through this shop which acted as the postal agent for the area and was handed the fat letter.

As Nyaradzai left the shop, a kaleidoscope of her life back at her village was playing through her mind. After their father died, their mother did not remarry. I do not want to give the girls the huge problem of getting used to a step-father, that is how she explained it. She vowed to look after her twin daughters single-handedly and therefore she established a market stall at their growth-point and sold vegetables and fruits to travellers in buses that passed through the small place. The girls went through primary school and it was when they were doing their third-year secondary school that they parted ways the way two pathways suddenly diverged in a deep dark forest. Nyaradzai remembered vividly the third year at secondary school perhaps because it was only less than a year ago or because it was during it that their lives changed remarkably. Nyaradzo fell in love with a young teacher who came to teach at their school. Although this was not allowed in the education system, she did not regret that love affair. In the two weeks that she had known him, the teacher had shown that he was so caring and very benevolent; he gave her whatever she asked for. He had already bought her a phone and some clothes and was even talking about paying fees for both of them at the school. Their mother was very grateful for this too. When other villagers advised her to report what was going on between her daughter and the teacher she put sticks into her ears so that she does not hear what they were saying.

One Sunday Nyaradzai borrowed Nyaradzo's dress. She wanted to go to church. The church was being held in one of the classrooms at the school that they attended. Nyaradzai did not want to go since she was down with flu. Since they shared lots of other things, Nyaradzo did not mind lending her the dress. It was the dress that her teacher-boyfriend had bought her the previous week. The service went through its paces and in one and a half hours it was over. The congregation went their separate ways.

"Nyaradzo!" Someone was calling from one of the classrooms.

Nyaradzai looked that way. She saw her sister's boyfriend, Gomba, beckoning to her through the window. She left the other girls and went to see him. The other girls continued walking home slowly waiting for her to catch up.

"I didn't think you would come to church since you said you had flu," the man said as he quickly hugged her and kissed her at the same time.

"But I'm not ..." she could not find space to tell him that she was not Nyaradzo. The man was all over her right there in the classroom; sucking her breasts, unzipping his trousers, stripping her panties, and before she knew it, he was on top of her groaning like a wounded buffalo.

After that encounter she skipped a period and in two months she realised that she was pregnant. She told the man responsible. The man did not deny it but he negotiated with Nyaradzai's mother so that the issue would not be reported. He was ready to welcome Nyaradzai as his wife. Since they were identical he had no problem with that. The girls' mother did not want to upset the set-up so far. She knew she was going to benefit a lot from the young teacher especially when the economy of the country was in the ICU, as the people described it.

That was how Nyaradzai left school to go and live with her sister's boyfriend's family in the eastern district of the country. Since then she had not gone back; going back would have exposed the man who was their benefactor. It was through phone calls and messages that she learnt of the transfer of Nyaradzo to a school in the city. Nyaradzo's mother feared that what happened to

44

Nyaradzai could also happen to Nyaradzo if she kept attending the same school.

When Nyaradzai arrived home, the sun was hurrying to bury itself behind the jagged hills in the western horizon. Her mother-in-law was busy preparing supper. Nyaradzai was lucky to have such a loving woman for a mother-in-law. Little did the mother-in-law know that she was not the actual daughter-in-law she was meant to have. She often excused her from doing strenuous work and often told her that, as the baby she was carrying was her first grandchild, it was important that she rested and let it grow well. There was warm water in the bucket that was always on the fireplace. Nyaradzai poured some into a bath tub and went out to bath. When she came back food was ready to be served. That day she did not spend much time in the kitchen hut. She quickly went to her bedroom. She was anxious to read the letter that Nyaradzo had sent to her.

After she had changed into her night-dress and had brought the mosquito-net down, Nyaradzai took the fat envelope and opened it carefully since it was tightly packed the way an egg is full of egg-stuff. Nyaradzai drew the paraffin lamp closer to her bed and lying on her back began to read the letter:

*I'm writing this letter to let you know how I feel about the life that has been thrust upon us, not because we chose it but because we were born similar and of the same mother. My sister, I've come to realise that everything that has happened to you is because of me and also that what is happening to me right now is also a result of my confusion and bad choices that I've made in my life. Therefore, I ask you to forgive me for all the pain I've caused you.*

*I grew up beside you not knowing that we could ever be different because we are like biscuits baked from the same mould. I'm so sorry to think that you had to take my place due to our likeness. I really loved Gomba with all my heart and I know that you hated him even before you became involved with him and even as you read this letter you still haven't fallen in love with the father of your baby. But what could we do? You were pregnant and I wasn't. If ever it was possible to transfer the pregnancy from you to me, just like the way we did with our shoes or dresses, I would have willingly done that with you. But no, it's you who have to carry his baby and become his wife. If it wasn't for Mother who did not want you to abort that pregnancy, everything would still be as it was in the beginning and I wouldn't have fallen into the pit that I am in right now. I wish you all the best with him.*

*When you were sent there, where you are, Mother decided that I should change schools. Therefore, she asked her brother, our only uncle, who stays here in the big city to take me in so I can finish school. She was not sure that I could attend school where my brother-in-law was teaching without me falling in the same trap you happened to fall. Mother didn't want to lose twice, or to have one son-in-law from her two girls. So, a month after you left I was sent here where so many strange things can happen and no one really cares. The people in the city are what I've come to call Halfricans. Because this place is a boiling pot of many cultures, religions and beliefs, people can do what they feel is right for them. While back at home we used to oh ah when we saw women wearing trousers, here I've met girls and women who boast that they don't have a single dress in their wardrobes and that it doesn't bother them a bit. I'm still in shock every time I see men and women walking hand in hand and kissing right in front of me. Sometimes I think I'm having those dreams that we always wished we could wake up from and pretend we never dreamt them. But beyond that, little did I know that men could marry other men and women could also marry each other. Then I'm reminded of Sodom and Gomorrah. And that is exactly what has happened to me.*

*You'll agree with me that the two of us, you and me, are well-built and beautiful girls. I know this because many boys were always saying it when we were still together in that school back home. I hope you still remember that boy whom we shared when we were in primary school. Although I loved him very*

46

much that did not take away my feelings for you. Today I'm not sure whether they were sisterly feelings of love or what I have had to experience here in the city. One day I was sent by Uncle Chake to the shops to do some shopping. While I was standing in the check-out queue this lady started chatting me up. She talked about many things that are happening around especially for young school girls like me. At first, I didn't pay much attention to her but when she spoke about getting a job during the holidays I got interested and we exchanged numbers so we could communicate.

No later than a week later she called me.

"Nyaradzo, I've to see you."

She asked me to meet her in town. I had never been in town. She then offered to meet me at the shop where we had met the first time. She turned up in a big car with four O's in front that are linked. I've seen this car before but when I first met this lady in the shop, I didn't think she could own such a car. When she asked me to jump in I first had to stump my feet on the tarred road so that I don't go inside with the township dust that clung to my false leather Chinese shoes. Inside was a strong and luxuriant perfume that clung in the air as if it could be touched. Everything inside was gleaming and the leather seats squeaked when I sat on them. I felt like I was a piece of dirt that should be swept out.

"You're looking stunning today," she said as she eased the big car back into the thick Friday afternoon traffic. I could not believe that she was saying that.

By now my head was turning and swirling due to the stereophonic music that was playing in the car. It wasn't loud but it was rich and because it came out of four speakers that surrounded us that's why my head started doing what it was doing. We drove downtown and she showed me places that I didn't know existed in this country. After that she said I needed grooming. That's where everything started. I didn't understand that word until she took to a hairdresser. When I came out of there my hair and nails were done in such a way that Uncle Chake was surprised when he saw me later that day. When he asked me

47

*about it, I told him that your husband had sent me some money for that but he wasn't satisfied. He wanted to call you to find out but I lied to him that I don't have your number.*

*When I met Tendai the following day, I told her about it and she said she would help me. Help me how? I didn't know and she couldn't say how she was going to help me. Uncle Chake was very angry when he saw me wearing new clothes which Tendai had bought for me.*

*"Nyaradzo, tell me dear daughter of my sister, where are you getting the money that you're splashing on yourself like this? Do you have a boyfriend already?"*

*I was very angry and arrogant. Why should he ask me about where I got the money to buy myself clothes? Why didn't he mind his business? Moreover, he had not even bought me a pair of slippers since I had started living under his roof for all these months. His wife was even mean with her food. We shouted at each other and exchanged insults that I didn't even know I could create. Later, I told Tendai about it and she asked me to come and stay with her. She also said she would meet all my needs and expenses. So, I had to say goodbye to Uncle Chake and start to stay with Tendai.*

*Life then was beautiful. She has a house in the leafy low-density suburbs. Suburbs have bigger houses and are quieter than in the township where Uncle Chake lives. I continued attending the township school. Tendai promised to transfer me to one of the elite schools in the suburb where we are living at the end of the following term. She drives me to school every morning as she goes to work. Since then I've not been to visit Uncle Chake and his family. This new life has grabbed me by the throat and threatens to strangle me.*

*Before the rut I'm in now I couldn't wait for the weekend to come. The books and everything associated with school stayed far from me when it was a weekend. My partner took me and still takes me to spend weekends at the most expensive holiday resorts in the city. We share the same hotel room and sleep on the same bed even at home. Sometimes I want to use 'our' for everything because I have become part of her. I'm the mistletoe growing on her and feeding from her and she also enjoys me a lot. I'm still young and beautiful and full of life. She complements me profusely all the time.*

*Our bedroom, in that four-bedroomed house, cannot be compared to any that I know of. It would have been more appropriate if I were to send you a video clip of the room. It is such a big room that it can fit two king size beds leaving enough space to place a dressing table and a two-seater leather couch. On the wall, opposite the headboard, hangs a 60" Samsung UHD television. We often watch soapies and videos while reclining on the huge down pillows that cover half the bed. I know that some of these things are strange to you as much as they were to me before I entered this kind of life. There is a built-in jacuzzi where we take baths with bathing salts. I'm not sure if you know what a jacuzzi is because I only came to know it when I fell in love with Tendai. You should see my complexion these days. You'll be surprised, mumwe wangu. Many times, I ask myself whether I'm dreaming or not, but the reality of life smacks me in the face when I go to school where I mingle with my school mates coming from poor backgrounds where their parents scratch around to put together a decent meal daily on the table.*

*There are so many things that I've learnt. At the beginning of all this I thought, yes, having a relationship with another woman is the best thing ever. But since last week things haven't been as usual. Tendai came from work and said:*

*"I want to say something to you."*

*That's how she begins all the time when she has something new to tell me.*

*"I'm so happy to have you here as my lover. All these days I've cherished our relationship and I must say you're amazing. I've decided to establish a small investment just for you. Just in case."*

*I was surprised to hear this. In case of what? She went on to tell me that she was going to rent out two rooms and the money from there would go towards my university education. As you know I've two more years before I go to varsity so I was ecstatic about this news. I jumped with joy. I kissed and sucked her like I've never done before. She said she would take me to the bank so that I* can open an account in which the tenant who will come to stay with us will deposit the rent money each month. That night I made love to her with abandon.

During that week, after work, Tendai was always on the phone answering calls from prospective tenants. She said she had put an advert in the papers to announce the availability of two rooms at our house. By Wednesday evening people started trickling in to view the rooms and to be interviewed. The person who eventually became our tenant is an athletic young man of about twenty-five. His name is Farai. We share the kitchen, lounge and the common bathroom with him. Something about this man unsettles me right from the first time I set my eyes on him. He reminds me very strongly of Gomba. His smile, his eyes, his body structure, the way how he walks and even his voice – everything about him is similar to your husband. By now I'm sure you're familiar with the humility and kindness that is in your man. It's unfortunate that our likeness confused him and he took you for me. Well, what could he have done? Moreover, it was only a fortnight since I had fallen in love with him. This is not sitting well with me. It is stirring in me a lot of memories and feelings that I had forgotten about.

In the few days that he has been with us he has encouraged me to run with him on Sundays. He says it is important to run to maintain my slim body structure. The other day we did ten kilometres. He says we must increase the frequency of our runs to be fitter. Farai is also helping me with homework every evening. My performance at school has actually improved. While Tendai wasn't interested in helping me with homework, Farai has taken it upon himself to ask me if I've any homework to do every day. Even Tendai is pleased with this turn of events. Like I said above, this man has revived those feelings that I had suppressed all this time. Now I'm as confused as a cockroach in a burning cupboard. To tell you the truth, I had stopped looking at men and feeling what I used to feel when Gomba was near me or when he touched me. I had started looking at other women and erotic feelings would go rioting in my body. Every time I'm alone with him, and these times are many, I fight the temptation to *hug him and to do those things I used to do with Gomba in the little time that our love had flourished. I'm not sure whether Farai knows that I've a demon that I'm fighting with every day.*

*You're the only person I'm telling this. My friends at school do not know anything about what I'm going through. I can't trust anyone. There are people here who do not tolerate transsexual people. Several women have been raped by men saying that that will make them to start loving men. Some have even been murdered for being gay or lesbian especially in the townships. So, I want you to help me make up my mind. While my mind tells me not to abandon Tendai, my body has other thoughts that are driven by awakened feelings for Farai. I don't want you to reply to this letter because it might fall into the hands of Tendai. I don't want to spoil everything before I know where I'm standing. I shall call you when she is not at home and then we'll talk about this. Keep your phone charged all the time.*

*I'm hoping that the baby is growing well and is almost due. Greet Gomba when he comes to see you at the end of the month as he has always done.*

*Your loving sister*
*Nyaradzo.*

Nyaradzai released a long sigh when she finished reading the letter. She folded the letter and replaced it back into the envelope. Life is cruel, she thought as she turned to lie on the other side so that she does not press hard on her bulging tummy. For a long time, her mind remained blank. Outside a donkey brayed and a dog barked as if answering the donkey. The first thought that wormed into her mind was a question: how can a woman love another woman as if she is a man? She loved her sister and her mother, but she had never thought of loving them beyond the boundaries that her sister had revealed in the letter she had just finished reading. Perhaps these were her relatives but even with females she was not related to, she had never been attracted to them sexually like that.

She imagined how two women can enjoy sexual intercourse but try as she may, her imagination could not put together such a scenario. Furthermore, she had never heard that people of the same sex can get married and make a family.

# Chapter 6: The Eye Sore

His eyes are red like someone who smokes *dagga* every day. They are frightening and glowing like embers that have been stirred to ignite an almost dead fire. His nostrils flare out like those of a donkey that has mistakenly eaten a pod of hot pepper and, from them, two jets of foul breath are spoiling my air. There is a thick smouldering cigar clamped between his yellowing teeth. It smells like the cigarette I once found our neighbour sharing with his friend behind his shack the other day. I clearly remember that after smoking that cigarette, they coughed like motorcycles running out of petrol. Now in this man's hands is a large pair of scissors – the kind that is used by the caretakers to trim the hedge at my school. I see him now coming to me opening and closing the scissors, snapping the foul air in-between in a scary way.

I look into his red eyes trying to read what his intention is but it is difficult because of the smoke that is curling around his head and his heavily bearded face. One thing that I am sure of is that he is up to no good and as such I am moving backwards trying to get as far away from him as possible. But his stride is longer than mine. He is gaining on me quickly. My right heel kicks a stone half embedded in the dusty road and I fall on my back. Now I am looking at him from where I am lying down on my back. He yanks off my khaki shorts in one swift move, grabs my small balls with his left hand the way one would squeeze a 2kg sugar plastic bag full of water. Then with his right hand he brings his scissors slowly towards my groin. My skin is crawling all over.

"*Maiwe-e!*"

"What is it, Tammy?" Mother's voice pierces the morning silence from the kitchen-room of our shack.

I wake up. Sweat is streaming down my forehead like water flowing down the rocky summit of a mountain after a thundery afternoon shower. My sleepy eyes are stung by the morning sunlight beaming through the un-curtained rectangular hole which functions as the window. I have to squint them to get them used to the light. I also knead them with my balled hands like a cat waking up from an afternoon nap, to speed up their adjustment.

At that moment, the door flies open and Mother comes in, water dripping from her wet fingers.

"Why are you screaming like that, Tamai?"

I do not answer immediately. My heart is still drumming from the fright that I had gone through a few moments ago. I look around trying to find out if the man with the pair of scissors was really there in the room.

"H– he wa-wanted t-t-to cut me with a pair of scissors." I stammer. Unseen ants still crawl over my skin.

"Who is he?" Mother's face is worried. She has never wanted anyone to hurt me. She loves me. I am her only child. She has often fought my battles against bigger boys who bullied me. Father left us four years ago when he went to another country because he had lost his job on the farms when the 'children of the soil' claimed their land from the white farmers. Since then he has not come back and we have not heard anything about or from him.

"A big bad man, mama. He wanted to cut me here." I point at my groin shy to tell her that the man wanted to remove my testicles with the pair of scissors.

"Dreaming again? Was it a dream?"

I am not sure yet if it was a dream. I'm looking everywhere: at the floor, at the roof and behind our clothes hung on a wire line

54

because we do not have a wardrobe and behind the door. The man is not there. So he surely was in my head.

"Don't worry, my child. You're not cut at all." She takes me into her arms and brings me close to her warm body. I crush into her abundant bosom and do not want to separate from her for a while.

"Now, go to the bathroom or you'll be late for school." She tells me softly but firmly.

Mother releases me from her comforting embrace. From a nail on the other side of our bedroom I unhook a small towel and pick a slab of green soap from the upturned box that serves as our dressing table. There is a cracked mirror that stands on this table. I look at myself in it. Mother has often told me that I look like Father. On many occasions, I have taken a photograph of him that Mother keeps in the big suitcase under the bed and tried to look for these similarities but I have found none at all.

The bathroom is a makeshift one. It is an enclosure next to this shack that we call 'house'. It is made of hessian sacks tied to a frame of poles. It is mainly for bathing but when it is night time we can go in there to urinate because the communal toilets are far from this part of the informal settlement. It is such that when it is a hot October day, the whole suburb is engulfed in a strong stench of urine coming from these establishments.

When I get in there, I find a Chinese-made plastic dish full of steaming water. Mother always boils bath water for me in winter. She does not want me to bath in cold water. She wakes up around 4 o'clock and makes the fire to boil the water before she takes a kombi to the big market near the city centre to bring back tomatoes, onions, cucumbers, *rugare* and fruits that she sells at the roadside market in the settlement. This is how we have survived all these years since Father left.

I take off my vest and hang it on the wire that has been put there for the purpose. My shorts follow it there. I have no underwear: it was a luxury that I never dreamt of. After a long spate of urination, which is quite enjoyable, I start the ritual of taking the bath. I throw water over my head and then lather the short hair that is there with the green soap. I hate this part of my bath because sometimes water gets into my eyes and the stinging soap is not welcome in them. I scrub my head with my fingers to remove the dirt that maybe stuck there. My teacher runs her fingers through our hair daily at assembly to check whether we wash our hair regularly or not. If found with dirt, she pours a whole bucket of freezing water on you and you will spend the whole day in class shivering like a mangy dog.

My eyes are closed. I am engrossed in the business of washing my head when I hear a drone coming from the direction of the only 'road' that serves our settlement. This road comes out of the main road that leads to the international airport. Generally, there are no cars that come to our settlement because we are all poor people. Very few people have jobs and those who work earn very little to have the luxury of buying a car. The only cars that visit us are police vans when there is someone to be arrested or an ambulance when someone is terribly sick. Rarely do cars come to this place in the morning but, there, I hear the sound of an engine approaching us. The sound is growing louder and louder by the minute. I am wondering what this sound could be. As time slowly crawls by, I get the feeling that the sound is not of one vehicle. It sounds as if there are two or three vehicles approaching. Now I can hear residents shouting to each other as if passing a message. I cannot hear properly what they are saying because of the pitch of the vehicle noises. I stop scrubbing my head to listen.

"Tamai, come out quickly." Mother's voice is anxiously loud.

56

I take the dry towel and wipe my face. "What is it, Mother?"

I am struggling to get into my shorts. Some soapy water from my hair has streamed into my eyes and it stings irritatingly.

"They have come with bulldozers this time."

"Mother!" I had to call her three times. She could hardly hear me in the increasing noise. "Who is coming with bulldozers?"

"The government."

I can see wells of tears in Mother's anxious eyes. I do not understand. Why would Mother want to cry because the government was coming with bulldozers? I have heard government people on radio saying that their government was by the people and for the people. It had been chosen by the people and was there to do the wishes of the people, the speakers on radio had gone on to explain. I look around at the neighbouring shacks. Everyone is out and looking in the direction where the yellow bulldozers are approaching from. Some are busy bringing out their possessions – rickety tables, chairs, suitcases bursting with clothes and kitchen things. These people could have had a similar experience from the year 2005 when Operation Murambatsvina was carried out on illegally built houses. I was not born yet but Mother has often told me about it.

The big noise of the approaching bulldozers is now threateningly loud. I can feel my insides jarring due to the sound. Their bucket-size exhaust pipes belch dark smoke that is added to that from our own wood fires. This cloud of smoke hangs over our shanty-town like a cloud of locusts which is about to descend on the ground for an overnight rest. Following behind the bulldozers are three trucks full of policemen wielding glass shields and batons

A few of these men have guns – probably teargas-canister launchers.

We stand there and watch them approach. I must be looking like I have been dragged in dirty water because soapy water still drips from my head. I am wearing shorts only. The bulldozers have disrupted everything. I could have finished my ablutions by now and would be tucking in my breakfast, but as I see it, I am considering school as having been cancelled. And speaking of school, there is no school in our plastic and cardboard shanty-town. We have to walk about four kilometres to attend school in a proper suburb which is to the east of the airport.

Mother is confused. I am confused. Everyone around us is confused.

"Why are the bulldozers coming here? Do they want to do roads for us? And look, they are being escorted by policemen." I point to the security personnel carriers full of policemen following slowly behind the loud-mouthed monsters. Mother follows where I am pointing with her eyes.

The monsters are now at the edge of our suburb. They have already moved out of the road that leads to the international airport. We no longer can hear the humming of traffic to and from there. The monsters are moaning and droning like hungry monstrous creatures ready to maul everything in their way. Everyone is now standing outside their dwelling gaping at the machines not knowing what is going to happen. I can smell the spent diesel fumes from those chimney-like exhaust pipes. They stop as they enter our stadium where we play soccer with plastic balls at the end of each day. The personnel carriers drive past them and stop. A smaller police van (which I have not seen) comes away from the back of the fleet and proceeds into our shanty town.

"Residents of Garikai," the booming loudspeaker on top of the small van disturbs the silence of the settlement. "The government has given you a very long time to move away from here and it seems you have not bothered to do so. Therefore, you're to be forcibly removed. You have been warned several times to go back where you came from but you are obstinate. Today we will see who is stronger: you or the government. If you don't remove your things from those shacks, the bulldozers will destroy them together with the shacks. Any resistance will be met with teargas and batons."

Mother looks down on hearing these words. Is she going to cry? I am trying to read her face but she does not look at me or up. By now all the flurry about going to school has been suspended. I am gripped by the mystery of the presence of the bulldozers and the police. I am thinking of the picture I am going to draw when I go to school next time. It would show the bulldozers raving up into our shanty town and the police standing stupid behind their glass shields in the lorries wielding the black batons. In my Grade R class I am well known for drawing pictures of what happens in my neighbourhood. I once drew a picture of the opposition party leader shouting a slogan with his open hand when he came to address us at the beginning of this year. My teacher refused to put it on the display board. She said it could get her into trouble with the police if they were to see it. I was confused.

"We are giving you thirty minutes to take out your things from those shacks." The loudspeaker fills every corner with its voice again. I am sure even the rats that are our unwelcome housemates could hear and understand this. I could see one or two of them coming out of their hiding places, whiskers twitching and trying to make sense of the situation.

The waiting is not long. Soon the bulldozers are raved up. A long thick chain is fixed to the two bulldozers. Then they move away from each other to stretch out the chain and are approaching one section of our suburb with the chain in-between them. I am not sure of what they are up to. As they sidle towards the shacks I see behind them another machine which I learnt later that it is called a digger. It has a long arm in front that is similar to the front legs of a praying mantis. It can swing this one arm in whatever direction the driver wishes it to swing. Next time I am going to get my hands on some wires I will be making a resemblance of this funny machine. All in all, it is fascinating watching the three machines as they swing into action.

The bulldozers, with the one-hundred-metre-long thick chain in-between them, slowly approach our shacks. Some of the people have finished removing their meagre belongings and are standing away from the path of the two bulldozers as if they are would-be sojourners waiting for a bus at a roadside bus stop. I can see rickety tables swinging in the morning air, backless chairs with torn seat pads, old sofas picked from dumpsites, old mattresses stained with the urine of delinquent babies or drunken fathers, some black handles of pots poking out of hessian sack-bundles like cow horns; there are suitcases dating back from the 60s and the 70s almost bursting with old clothes and blankets.

Some of our people are not at home. Their shacks are still locked with everything that belongs to them inside.

My age-mates are near the bulldozers now, curiously following them as the machines approach the houses. They are having fun seeing those monstrosities at close quarters. Mother has forbidden me from joining them. She is afraid that I might get lost in the confusion that she thinks is going to follow. I hate Mother for doing this to me. I need to see these machines at close quarters for the benefit of drawing them accurately when I go to school.

The chained-linked bulldozers are now near the dwellings. The heavy chain, having brought down a few small trees at the edge of the settlement, scythes one of the shacks and the roof comes down on top of the remains of what had been the walls. From how my friends are shrieking and running around I can see that they are chasing after rats which are fleeing the destroyed building. More structures are coming crushing down as the bulldozers move along. Behind them the digger is busy knocking down whatever the chain was unable to level down. Red dust is rising up into the morning air as if a dusty-devil is passing through the settlement.

Now the bulldozers are approaching the shack of the Silent One. I cannot remember the owner of this shack speaking to anyone in the shanty-town. Perhaps that is the reason why people called him the Silent One. No one knows his name. No one knows where he came from to be here living with us. Most of us know where we came from. We came from the white people's farms after the people had taken 'their soil'. Our lives had been tied to the farms but when the 'children of the soil' had come to wrestle it from the settlers, Father and Mother and others lost their jobs. Therefore, the only places where we were welcome were the outskirts of cities and towns. Mother says we are from a country to the east. Our ancestors came to this country many, many years ago when people were shading skins and putting on cotton-cloth clothes. We had no rural-areas-of-origin as default home areas to go to. This is how Garikai had sprung up right here on the red soils east of the big city.

The Silent One bothers no one and no one, in turn, bothers him. But recently the Silent One had not been seen in Garikai. His cabin has been locked for a week now. Since he bothers no one, no one cared about his coming and going. As the chain between the machines scrapped the ground towards the Silent One's shack we all stood there wondering if people should have broken his door to save his belongings like they had done with the others who were not around.

As we watch the bulldozer flattening the shacks, no one anticipates what happens before the chains hit the Silent One's cabin. A swarm of bees buzzes angrily out of a hole in the door of the shack. They are so many that we can see them flying out like a small grey cloud from where we are standing. They attack the drivers of the bulldozers who jump down from the bulldozers leaving them standing there punting and puffing like elephants bogged in mud. They attack the police men in their eggheads standing behind their glass shields. The drivers run wildly towards the police personnel carriers. Their hands are flailing above their heads in a frantic bid to drive away the mad bees. The policemen who have been walking besides the bulldozers as they flattened the shacks have thrown their glass shields away and are running around like ants whose nest has been unwittingly disturbed by a herd of cattle.

Everyone is surprised by what is happening. Children, like me and the others, find it a lot comical to see the adults running like mad men chasing shadows, leaving their lorries behind, running, beating the air besides their heads with their open hands, their boots thudding on the ground. Some of them remove their egg-heads and throw them away because the bees are getting inside. We laugh and roll ourselves in the red dust. Our parents are not amused by all this. I don't know why. Could it be because the red dust that we are rolling in would stick to our khaki clothes and be a problem on a washing day and they are worried about? They look at us with talking eyes, but we don't want to understand that kind of language now. Instead we choose to crack our ribs with laughter as we watch the drama unfolding before us.

*

62

After four days, the bulldozer crew and the police are back. They are accompanied by the people from the wildlife department who specialise in capturing bees. It is a Saturday. We have not gone to school. So, we have the opportunity to watch what is happening. The police help the bulldozer drivers to refuel their machines while the bee-catchers go to the Silent One's shack. The bulldozers were left running by the drivers for four days and the fuel in their tanks ran out. We are standing at the safety of our mothers' shacks looking at the unfolding scene with interest. The bee-catchers, looking like space travellers in their plastic suits and visors, advance towards the shack shaking from the fear of the mysterious bees they have heard of and had come to remove so that the demolition of our settlement can go ahead. Government is really determined to uproot us from where we have been staying since 2011 when the 'children of the soil' had taken our boss's farm.

The bee-catchers approach the shack cautiously. Not a bee has come out to investigate them. They look around the shack trying to locate the entrance through which the bees go in and out of the shack. They have gone around the shack several times the way goats do when they are scratching themselves on the walls of a hut. This tells us that they haven't found the entrance-cum-exit for the bees. One of them produces a pair of cutters and breaks the chain that secured the door of the shack. When the door of the shack is flung open, we all expect a swarm of bees to burst out and start to sting the intruders, but nothing like that happens. Cautiously, the man who has cut the wire securing the door enters the one-roomed structure and we hear him rummaging inside like someone looking for something. Shortly he comes out. From where we stand we cannot hear what their verbal exchange is but from the men's gestures, Mother can tell that the man did not find any bees inside the shack. The man does not bother to close the door of the shack, instead the two of them go where the drivers of the bulldozers have just finished refuelling the machines and have successfully brought them back to life again.

One of the policeman takes out a megaphone. He climbs on top of the police van before he speaks into it: "Residents of Garikai, we would like to advise you to take out your belongings from your shacks. We would like to finish off what we left unfinished four days ago. Be quick about it. We've no time to waste here today."

Mother looks at me as if she is seeing me for the first time. Her eyes are misting with tears. I know she cries easily. She must be thinking of where we will go from here. Perhaps she is not the only one going through such thoughts. However, the revving sounds of the bulldozers spur her into action. She goes inside our shack to remove our property. I am also going to help with that.

"I don't know what to do, my child. I wish your father was here for us. He is the one who brought us here in the first place." She says as she wipes her cheeks with the end of the green apron tied around her waist.

I look at her in the face. I want to tell her that everything is going to be alright but I do not know how. I am only a child; I have never read a manual of how adults work. Perhaps if I act like a man she would know, so, without hesitation I shoulder butt the door and start bringing our more of our belongings out of the shack and handing them to her. Mother is piling them a few metres away. We do not have much though. Soon we are standing beside our property: a wooden bed with a mattress with maps of the countries of the world from my urine when I was much younger, two pots and several plates, an old garden chair which my father had been given by his boss at the farm, a canvas bag in which are our blankets and clothes – that was that! We watch the bulldozers as

64

they raze down the rest of Garikai. Everything is flattened and the rats are running here and there trying to find some hiding places among the rubble and plastics.

Then, from the big city direction, we see a cloud of red dust rising in the air. Soon a fleet of seven lorries has arrived at our ruins. The same policeman who spoke through the megaphone previously climbs on top of the van again.

"Former residents of Garikai, your government has sent these seven lorries that you see here for your transport. I'm advising you to load your belongings into any one of them and you will be taken to a place much better than this one."

On hearing this people pick up their beds, their bundles of blankets, their pots and pans, their chairs and tables and throw them into the nearest lorry. A few rats and some cockroaches, some hidden in the old sagging sofas and others in cupboards with doors hanging on their hinges, are loaded into the lorries. There is a frenzy of excitement that galvanises the people of Garikai into action. They run around like ants on a summer afternoon trying to plug their holes just before a rain shower. When everything is safely in the lorries we climb on top of broken property, bags of clothes and blankets, cardboard boxes of plates and pots and wait to be driven to this new place which has been described as being better than Garikai.

When everyone is on board, the lorry drivers jump into their cabins and our journey to the unknown new settlement begins. Later on, we were to learn that we had been removed from there because we were an eyesore. People arriving in the country were first greeted by our desperate situation so we had to be hidden away from foreign visitors.

# Chapter 7: Used Condoms

The smell of early summer wafted into the stuffy bus through the half open windows. It came from the forest of *muzhanje* trees through which the dusty road threaded: wet earth, wild *mazhanje* and new leaves exuded their aromatic smells that filled the noses of everyone in the old bus. The season promised to be a good one compared to the previous one which had almost been a disaster. The elders could tell this from the abundance of *mazhanje*, the direction of the first winds, the arrival of the first black and white storks and swallows.

I sat at the back of the bus counting the multi-coloured campaign posters strapped to the trees alongside the road. It was that time of the year when politics, like cholera or malaria, took to the roads, farms, rural areas, towns infecting everyone. Politics, like ticks clinging to the udder of an old cow, was on the mouths of everyone since national elections were due in March of the following year. As usual when I have a bus journey to do, a big beer bottle would be nestled between my knees in a bid to shut out all the unnecessary chattering that would go around me.

"They were used like condoms, that's what my history teacher told us." The girl in the seat in front of me told the boy sitting next to her. They spoke on top of their voices, excited that the year was over and they were going home for the festive holiday.

"My father was one of them. Today, thirty-four years after the war, he has nothing to show for all the scars he gathered during the war." The boy looked at the girl. I would have loved to see their expressions as they said all this but, unfortunately, I was sitting behind them.

"Do you know what they were called?"

"Who doesn't? *Mujibha*s and *chimbwido*s. They were the scouts of the freedom fighters. They did all the dirty work: organizing *pungwes*, killing sell-outs and burying landmines and even raking battle areas. It's a pity they haven't been recognized as much as happened to freedom fighters who enjoy pensions while their children's school fees are paid for by the government."

It was early on the first Saturday of September 1979. I woke up to the sound of gunfire and thumping mortar bombs. We had heard these many times before, from a far-off distance, of course, but what I heard on that day was close by because I could hear the ground vibrating every time a mortar bomb went off. I crept outside to investigate where exactly the battle was taking place. It was just across Mupinge River. The lingering darkness, though being driven away by the approaching twilight, allowed tracer bullets to draw their curving blue, red and yellow trajectories across the greyish horizon. The light staccato of AK 47s and SKS rifles was punctuated now and again by the deep throated booms of mortar bombs. The sounds were frightening, they shook my bowels; flashes of light lit up the morning every time a bazooka bomb was fired and also when it exploded on the other side of the battle. I had never been that close to a battle before. It gave me a pounding heart.

I went back into my bedroom hut; my shirt and shorts were where I had thrown them last night - in an uncomfortable heap by the foot of the old handed down bed from my parents. I shoved my legs into my shorts and threw the shirt on my back. The early September mornings can be nippy. I emerged out of the hut. I knew that the freedom fighters would be arriving as soon as those guns went silent and we, that is, my fellow village youths and me, would be spending the day running errands and keeping surveillance for them. In the mean time I had to wait in readiness.

The 'boys' liked to spend the day time at our homestead because it was on a hill that gave a good view of the surrounding are. The place had become known as 'the highland'.

What did we, *vanamujibha*, not do for the 'boys'? We scouted and scoured the surrounding area for the presence of the Rhodesian forces. They would want us to count the soldiers, what arms they were carrying, how many were black and how many were white. We had to know where they were headed for and were they were going to spend the night. Sometimes they would send us to go plant landmines on the road that ran through the village. We went shopping for cigarettes and sweets for them. Our sisters, *vanachimbwido*, washed and ironed their uniforms, cooked for them and rumours had it that they sexually entertained them too although the 'boys' often preached celibacy and flatly denied this even though no one ever accused them of it.

I did not have long to wait. Before the red rising sun peeped over the eastern horizon, I saw dark figures with back packs fleeting among the trees near the cattle kraal. Soon they arrived breathing hard like they had been on a 21.1km run. They must have retreated and ran all the way across Mupinge River and then through the bush between the village and the river. They looked agitated and were always looking over their shoulders as if expecting to see whoever they had been fighting to appear and continue the battle. Their uniforms were torn and dusty and there were holes on their trousers at the knees. It would seem they had been crawling all the way from the battle field. Two had bandages on their arms seething with blood. As soon as they arrived in our yard they took positions around the home in pairs as was their

68

custom every time they camped. Their commander came to where I was waiting for them.

"Did you hear the guns?" He did not greet me at all. "We were killing the ZIPRAs on Farm 24 there. Stupid idiots!"

I was shocked. Questions of which I had no answers started to overwhelm my mind. So the ZANLAs had been up against the ZIPRAs. What was happening? Were these two armies not sharing the pungwe arena just a few days ago at Farm 18? Were they not singing Ndebele and Shona liberation songs together then? Were they not preaching the same word of a free and non-tribalism Zimbabwe? Did they not sit in posts and shared newspaper wrapped tobacco and dagga in the fringes of pungwe arenas? For over two months the two armies had been moving together and engaging a common enemy and urging us to support both of them.

So why were they fighting each other now?

Suddenly it occurred to me that we, the village youths, were at the shit-end of the war. This fall out between the ZANLAs and the ZIPRAs was going to be a big headache for us. What I could not understand is how we were going to receive the ZIPRAs when they come asking us to do what we had been doing for them in the last few months. We were at the centre of three armies, all fighting each other. The only side that I knew was friendly so far was that of the ZANLAs.

"Comrade Garikai!" The commander cut my thoughts short.

"Gather your fellow boys. I want you to go and look around where we've been fighting. Pick anything you will find there and bring it here. Also tell the girls to come here."

"Okay, *mukoma*."

First, I woke up my sister so she can gather the other village girls. I went to Jokoniya's place. He was already up. Together we took the road that led to Farm 24. By now the September sun was warming up our backs and shortening our shadows.

"What went wrong? Why did they shoot at each other?" Jokoniya said after I had told him what had happen across the river. He continued rolling his tobacco on a piece of *The Rhodesia Herald*.

"I don't know. Comrade Mambara didn't say much. And I'm not amused. I hope to hear more when we are back from our mission."

He scratched a match and a pungent cloud of smoke covered his head. The smell of raw tobacco invaded my nostrils. "What do you mean by that?"

"So you can't see the problem that we are going to have after all?"

Jokoniya looked at me through the smoke of his cigarette.

"We've been in problems since this war spilled into this district. What could be another problem?"

"If the ZIPRAs come tomorrow when the ZANLAs are gone how are we going to deal with them? If they are enemies now where do we stand? Remember we have no guns to defend ourselves." I looked at him meaning to make him appreciate my point of view.

"Obviously they have become our enemies. Anyone who messes with the ZANLAs messes with us."

"Now we've two enemies who we must look out for all the time. The ZIPRAs have been known to operate in the west of this country. All those stories that we've heard about them ..."

"I know, but we'll hear what *vanamukoma* are going to say about it all. They must advise us on what to do when they come. Maybe they will drive them where they came from."

We were now across the river. We went over the farm fence that separated the reserves and the small-scale farms. The brown

70

grass was up to our ears here because there were fewer cattle grazing it. The trees towered above us, their branches forming canopies that threatened to block out the sunlight. We waded through the tall grass; our heads just bobbing above it like the so-called Bushmen would have done in much shorter grass. We were nearing the proximity of the battle field now. I was afraid. My heart was thumping in my chest. I am sure Jokoniya's was doing the same. We were quiet now. The mission had to be seen through; we had to go and rake the battle field for the 'boys'.

As we approached the farm homestead, the grass started to thin out and to become shorter. The cattle and goats grazed here more often. Jokoniya was the first to notice something as we approached the homestead. He pointed at the bark of trees that had been chipped off. Some branches were hanging from their trees. These had been clipped by the bullets. As we cautiously inched further we started to see spent cartridges behind some trees where someone had taken cover while firing. Further on, Jokoniya pointed at a crater on the ground where a mortar bomb had exploded. A few metres from the crater Jokoniya picked an AK47 magazine full of bullets. We began to pick single bullets as we looked around. This made me feel very proud.

"Gari, come and see." Jokoniya whispered to me.

I tiptoed to where he was standing. "My God!" he whispered in a supressed strident voice. "Someone must have died here. Look at this patch of blood that has drenched the soil." I looked over my shoulders as if expecting someone to challenge us. "And see, he was pulled away."

I looked at the trail. It was probably made by the dead person's elbows and the lifeless head. There were drops of dried blood on the grass. We followed the trail. It crossed the road into the deeper forest to the west of the homestead. We turned back walking like

71

thieves intending to steal from an orchard. The place was very frighteningly quiet. The only sounds that disturbed the silence were those of the birds and the chickens that went on with their business of fending for food as if nothing had happened. I wondered where the people of this home were at that time. When would they come back to continue with their lives like the chickens?

As we entered the homestead we noticed another bloody patch of ground by the kitchen hut door. There were trails of elbows and a head as if the dead body had been pulled away by the legs. The walls of the main house were poked everywhere with bullet marks and some windows were shattered.

"Look!" I half whispered to Jokoniya showing him an AK47 rifle that had been abandoned next to the barn. It had no magazine on. I picked it up and examined it before I strapped it on my back as I had seen *vanamukoma* doing. We picked a few more rounds and another magazine.

"Shh! Listen!" Jokoniya put his index finger to his lips. From afar we heard the beat of helicopter rotors faintly wafting through the morning air. "There comes the dragon fly. Enough of this place. Let's go!"

We started off towards the river as if we were doing a 100m dash. As we ran I saw a rifle grenade lying in the grass. I stopped to pick it up and was soon behind Jokoniya. This was our territory; we knew all the nooks and crannies along the river. In a few minutes we were hiding in a cave that had been carved by flood water on the farm side of the river. Before we had breathed more than five times the helicopter breezed above us. We could see the helmeted white soldiers through the open door of the chopper. Its sound soon receded as it flipped over Chisungwa Hill to Manyame River ten kilometres to the west.

At about half past nine we trooped back to 'the highlands' almost in the same way *vanamukoma* had done earlier that day. We were panting like young dogs that had gone for their first hunt in the bush, but had only managed to smell out a dead carcass there. Like the small dogs we sought out the commander with what we had picked at the battleground. We proudly laid out our pickings: the thirty odd AK47 rounds, the two magazines, the AK47 rifle and the rifle grenade. The commander jumped away from us at the sight of the rifle grenade. We were surprised.

"Garikai, why did you pick that thing? Quick, get away from it!"

"But did you not tell me to pick anything we were to find at the farm?"

"No, no, no! You boys are lucky that grenade did not explode in your hands. That thing was fired but did not detonate, so it is dangerous as if it has just been fired."

At that moment of remembering these words, the bus hit a pothole with a loud bang. All the passengers were briefly thrown into the air. I shouted as if someone wanted to kill me. The bottle of beer that was in my hand crushed on the floor of the bus. I was shaking all over and sweat started pouring down my face. Everyone looked at me.

"What's the matter, *baba*?" The girl asked me as she moved away from me as if she had suddenly discovered that I had leprosy.

"I'm okay, I'm okay." I said repeating that like a fool. "Where are we now?" I asked her. I could see that she was not satisfied with what I had told her.

"Where are you getting off, old man?" The boy sitting next to her asked me.

"At Chigwada Store." I answered peering out through the window.

"We're past that shop, *mudhara*. We're at Mukwenya School."

I picked my satchel and hurried towards the door shouting, "Driver, stop here! Stop right here!" at the same time I was tugging at the bell rope to signal the driver to stop. I knew I had ten kilometres to walk back to my home.

# Chapter 8: Voices of the Ancestors

The October heat shimmers above the ground distorting the shapes of trees in the distance. Not a cloud can be seen in the blue hue of this dry season sky. Somewhere to the east a bushfire rages on. The smell of burning grass is in the afternoon air. Burnt ashes are carried to the west by the slight easterly that is prevailing during this time of the year; and these come down to land on everything, blackening it. Cicadas, for this is their time of the year, serenade the afternoon with a continuous shrill that lulls people to sleep. Sometimes the shrill is so incessant that it seems to be going on forever.

Nothing seems right for you at all. Your life is not what you expected it to be. The oppressive heat, the sweat rolling down the sides of your face and the troublesome flies are all a bother and an irritation and these make it even worse. The afternoon is long and drags by slowly as if time is about to stop. Perhaps it is the *sadza* and *kapenta* lunch that you have just had that makes you feel like that – tired. It is that kind of tiredness which makes you unable to brush the flies from your own eyes.

The baby on your lap starts crying. She whimpers like a puppy with a thorn in its paw. Your mind is drawn to her presence. You look at her. She is ten months old but not in prime health. She is malnourished and poorly looked after. Her ribs are sticking out. The tummy is extended unnaturally; her limbs are thin and appear not to be able to support the extended tummy; the whites of the eyes are yellowish like pus from a festering boil and the eyes themselves sit there in her sockets like two owl eggs that have just been laid in two separate nests. Her skin is so thin and delicate that sometimes you wonder how it is able to carry out its duties.

"Who is crying?" Your mother-in-law shouts from her bedroom hut. To you she sounds like someone speaking in a dream. Of late her speaking has turned into shouting.

"It's Mucha!"

"Why, so soon after lunch?"

"She's hungry. She couldn't touch the food."

Your mother-in-law shuffles to where you are sitting. She is shaking her head like someone trying to clear their mind. She is a wizened old lady whose presence disturbs you every time she comes to talk to you. She looks at you and you coyly look back at her. What you see in her eyes brings no peace to your tormented soul. That accusing look is still there and you cannot recall when it ever vanished from her eyes since the death of her son, your husband.

The child on your lap wriggles momentarily reminding you of a snake whose head has just been chopped off. You look at her thin limbs and sunken eyes. Your eyes glisten and out of habit you wipe them with the back of your left hand. You cannot fully understand what is happening to you and your child.

"What did you give her to eat?"

"This." You nod towards a bowl of the meal's leftovers by your side.

"My daughter," she says in a low forceful voice, "a baby needs far more than that. *Kapenta* and *sadza* every day is not good at all." She comes to sit near you. Her menacing presence overwhelms you and you wish you had never met her in your life.

"There's nothing to give variety to this food. The dam has dried and the gardens have died." In your mind you are saying, being a widow at my age makes the situation even worse. More tears well up in your eyes. Your face contorts and wrinkles line your forehead. If you had looked in a mirror you could have seen that it was like that of your mother-in-law.

Your mother-in-law sighs, looks at you and then away at the hazy mountain. "This is not my making. If I were you I wouldn't have allowed this."

These words coming from the old lady herself surprise you. Is she saying that I killed my husband? You ask yourself. Although you did not like to be Jorum's wife, you had done nothing to bring about his death. When you came to live with him weren't there signs of his illness? From the way he coughed and those night sweats which dampened the sheets you could tell that something was wrong with his health.

Muchaneta is now quiet. She is busy sucking her thumb. You look at her and once again you notice how she looks like her grandmother. You want to say something about that but you decide, at the very last moment, that it will serve nothing to mend the bridges between you and your mother-in-law.

You remember the first time you met Jorum. It was at his work place in the big city. His sister had taken you there. You had never been in the big city before and its lights had dazzled you so much that you had thought it alright to be his wife.

"So, this is the wife?" he snorted looking at you with an appraising eye just like a cattle buyer at a cattle sale does.

"Yes, brother," Mandinetsa said nodding at the same time as if to emphasise her answer. "The elders back home have agreed that you take her since your wife has died and you are the only one in the family who can have her as a wife."

"But... but I never said that I wanted a wife now, sister." Jorum retorted still surprised.

"Please don't argue with me. It's not me who decided that. The elders have only sent me to you with this girl. She is to be your wife." Mandinetsa looked at you and you looked shyly away. "If you're not in agreement with their decision they said you can come on your own and explain that before them. Remember that they summoned you several times to discuss the matter but you decided not to come."

"Didn't I explain to them that I am always busy here and would only come at Christmas?"

"Whatever you say, I've been sent to deliver your wife and, having done what I have come to do, please excuse me. I'll see you two when you come home for the holidays."

With those words Mandinetsa left the two of you standing there like strangers at a bus stop. Although Jorum showed his resentment at your coming, he did not regret your looks. Your simple rustic attire and style could be improved with a few hundred thousand dollars at a clothing store and hair salon.

At his lodging, at the outskirts of the big city, Jorum turned you into a woman and a wife at the age of fifteen. It was hard at first to live with a person you had never seen before, but as they say everything has a beginning. In two months' time Muchaneta was conceived. Then, like any girl brought up in the rural areas and now living in a big city, you considered yourself very lucky. Your friends, the ones you left at your father's village, were probably not married to men who worked in the big city. You cherished the idea of having been picked out of the poverty of the dusty village and being thrust into the affluence of the big city by circumstances beyond your influence. That made you forget those circumstances then.

"*Mai* Mucha," your mother-in-law draws your attention to the present. "I'll be back soon. There is a beer party across the river. I've been invited there."

You look at Muchaneta. She is sleeping. The thumb is still stuck in her mouth though she no longer sucks it. "What's for supper tonight, mother?"

Jorum's mother stands up and shakes her skirts. A few things drop from them. She looks at you and then at the looming hazy mountain to the north. "Catch that black cockerel and slaughter it. When I am back I wouldn't like to eat with those dried pumpkin leaves of yours."

With those words she fetches her snuff box from her bedroom hut and goes where the drum beat was beckoning. You watch her back as she walks away. Your mind races back to the time you used to live with your mother before this marriage. It is this thinking that stresses you most.

It was summer. You were coming from the river.

"Mother, why is it that you don't allow me to go and play with my friends?"

"Yes, my daughter. I will not do so because I must guard you against the boys of today."

"But mother, my friends are not those boys of today."

"I know. It's the girls who will drag you to the boys of today. You know what, I want you to grow into a beautiful maiden, unspoiled and well cultivated for marriage. The man who is going to marry you must thank me for looking after you well. He must pay me with a live cow for that."

"So, you don't trust me."

"No, my daughter, it's not that I don't trust you. The thing is every mother is worried about the future of her daughters. You see, I would like you to grow up and have a home like me, your mother."

These words disturbed you because you had not heard them coming from your mother's mouth before. Furthermore, you never thought your mother could say those words to you. You were very young then. Ten years was not an age when your ears could listen to such words.

"Sure enough," you had agreed. "But I don't see how I cannot do like what you have done."

"Out there, my daughter, there are men who want to destroy the lives of young girls like you. They are like snakes that bite what they do not eat."

The words of this discussion still echo in your head although it was a couple of years since they were said. On that day you decided not to shame your mother by doing things that would soil your name and spoil your future life. You wanted your mother to earn her live cow.

"Your father and I have never been shamed by your elder sisters. The three of them are married and busy building their families with their husbands."

"I'll not do anything besides what you expect of your daughters, mother." That was then, but now you are remembering such a discussion with remorse. Nothing has gone the way your mother wanted. Things have not gone the way you wanted too. All the promises and dreams have come to nothing.

Muchaneta stirs. She smiles in her sleep revealing the toothless gums that would soon be cracked as teeth sprout out. The sun is now low over the western horizon. You put Muchaneta on the reed mat and go to the granary to get grain to throw to the chickens so you can lure and catch the cockerel meant for dinner

\*

People of the villages are talking, and weeping, and mourning - morning, noon and night. A great sadness, as has never been witnessed before, has settled upon the countryside. Every day the substance of their talking, weeping and mourning remains the same: how they are burying their young loved ones every day. They also worry about the time they are spending at funerals rather than in their gardens tending their vegetables for food. The people's voices are sounding hurt by this. The questions that hang on their lips are: is this the end of the world? Has Armageddon finally caught up with the people? These are the questions that, like death, are haunting them as they move from funeral to funeral. Death lives among them now. It is no longer visiting like Christmas which visits once a year. It is not news to hear of a death in the villages anymore.

Speaking at one of the funerals, *Sabhuku* Choga had blurted, "My people, hear this: *Chose chinokwirwa chinouraya.*" This had confused his people – everything that is mounted can kill? Mounting a bicycle, a car, an aeroplane or a woman kills; was that what the village headman was saying? But some people who were dying were not doing so due to road accidents. The people chewed these words as they ate their dinners and drank their sorghum brews. They tried to get to the depth of their meaning but it took them a while. When they finally stumbled upon their meaning, women strongly disagreed with that. They argued that *kana zvinokwira zvacho zvave kuurayawo* – even those who mounted others were killers too. By this they meant that even the men who mounted them were as lethal as the women. Those who did not mind being labelled 'women with mouths where flies never landed' said that it took two people, a man and a woman, to court this kind of death. Many had gone away from that funeral shaking their heads because they did not think their village head would speak such words.

You, too, are not happy with what *Sabhuku* Choga said at that funeral. His message was not clear to you too, maybe this is the reason why you are not happy at the headman's words. If you knew what the old man was saying, you would not be unhappy but rather you would be frightened.

People are talking in their homes, in their fields, in their gardens – they are talking everywhere. You try to listen to this talk of their mouths but you cannot hear anything. The messages in their utterances are not meant for your ears because they are meant not to be heard by you. When you meet them, their eyes avoid yours because they are talking about you. You cannot meet their eyes with yours either. It is as if they are waiting for something nasty to happen to you, maybe a bolt of lightning descending straight from the blue skies and inflicting death on you at any time or the ground on which you stand to just open up and swallow you. This game of avoidance has been going on since the death of Jorum. The only person who does not seem to be in it is your mother-in-law, the mother of Jorum. She looks straight into your eyes and tells you directly that you are the cause of her son's death. It pains you to hear these words after all the care that you had given Jorum during his last days.

Sometimes you make up words that you think people are saying in their silence. You hear them saying that Jorum died of the new disease. If it takes one partner then the other must follow and it is only a matter of time before that happens. They are saying that you are next. This has sent shudders of fear down your spine. You are young. Your daughter, Muchaneta, is still a baby. You do not want to die and leave her without anyone to look after her. A thick tear drop rolls down your left cheek then another down the right one.

You are thinking of all this while you are sitting under the shade of the tree in the middle of the homestead. Like the day before, it is scorching hot. The air is thirsty. Your throat is parched and the water that you continue gulping down does nothing to help the situation.

But, today Muchaneta is much better. At least she is not crying or whimpering like the previous day. Perhaps it is because she has eaten well and suckled from a mother who ate well yesterday. The cock that you slaughtered was very delicious. Yes, very delicious because it had been a long time since you had chicken. Delicious also in the sense that the fat of the chicken still makes your lips smooth when you run your tongue over them. You no longer have to moisten them now and again.

You see a column of small black ants heavily laden with food. In your home area when a person sees a column of these tiny insects carrying food, it was said that he or she was going to eat some meat that day. This is what you grew up believing. Sometimes it turned out to be true. The small creatures are busy with their life right in front of you. You wonder whether any of the ants had problems in their lives like you. The supposedly quiet ants struggle under the weight of food as their column snakes its way into a hole at the foot of the tree you are sitting under.

"All alone as usual!"

You snap back to reality. Someone has spoken to you. You turn around and there is Chenjerai just entering your courtyard.

"No!" You defend yourself unnecessarily. "I'm not alone." Chenjerai's visits enlivens your spirit. "There is always Muchaneta with me here. How much company do you think a widow can afford?"

Chenjerai is a village mate and a friend who has always considered you a friend despite the fact that you are a mother and she is still unmarried. You placed her four or five years older than you.

"I know, my friend. The departed do not have anything to do with the living." She comes to where you are sitting. You sidle to the end of the mat to allow her sitting space on the reed mat.

Muchaneta stirs. She moans and yawns in her sleep. You pat her back and she heaves a deep sigh and retains her normal breathing and slips back into her afternoon sleep.

"How's she?" Chenjerai gestures at the baby.

"She's well, though she doesn't seem to be gaining any weight at all."

"You should take her to your mother. You know, you haven't gone back to your parents since you came here to marry the late Jorum."

"You think so?"

What Chenjerai is talking about takes you miles from where you are right now. You stare at the base of the tree. The column of the ants is not there anymore. They are probably finished with their day's work. A sense of loneliness drives you into a gloomy reverie. Your eyes moisten and instinctively you wipe them. In that spate of time your mind goes back many years ago.

It was after the death of one of your uncles, your father's elder brother. Your father had three brothers. You went into an unexplained trance which lasted a fortnight. Those who were there said that during that trance you said a lot of things that many people failed to understand. Your other uncles then decided to consult a *n'anga* on the death of their brother seeing that there was some link to what you were saying in your trance and the deaths. That was when the seed of your present predicament was sown. The *n'anga* told your father's brothers that their father, your grandfather, had murdered someone way back. The *n'anga* said that was the cause of the death of your uncle. The *n'anga* advised that there was need to compensate the family whose relative was killed by your grandfather if such deaths in the family were to be avoided. As tradition dictated a young girl was to be paid as compensation to the family whose member was murdered by your grandfather.

One day you over heard them talking about it. By this time you had come out of the trance. This thing was never discussed in your presence.

"Look, brother, you're the only one who has a young girl child. You can't let the family perish." One of your uncles pointed this out to your father.

"Not my child." Your mother had countered your uncle's suggestion.

"Shut up, you! You're only a *mutorwa* in this family. You were brought here to bear children for us." The uncle who had insisted on giving you away shouted at your mother. "We don't listen to women in this family."

"But look here, my brothers, this is the only child remaining in my family. Aren't there other ways we can settle this problem?" Your father tried to avert your uncles' demand for you.

"That's nonsense, *mukoma*. What you are saying shows that you're not one of us. Now how can we say we're a united family if you refuse with your daughter in order to save our family? I'm sure you'll be happy to see all of us, and even you, wiped away by this *ngozi*." That was the voice of your youngest uncle speaking.

Before your father could reply your mother chipped in and said: "I don't care about what you think about us *varoora*. I'm not going to let my child be given away to an unknown family as a way to stop this family from being wiped away by the *ngozi*. If anything like that is going to happen here I'll hang myself in this home and then you'll have two *ngozis* to deal with."

"No, Chenjerai. I cannot go back to my parents now." The present comes back. You do not tell her all that you have been

85

thinking. How can you tell her such secrets? This was the problem. The story of how you came to join Jorum's family is one secret that you do not like to tell people. People are bound to talk too much about it. This does not exclude even Chenjerai.

"And they have not bothered to visit you at all. Haven't you got a family?" Your thoughts fly away again. Images flash into your mind so vividly that you cannot flash them out. In your mind's eye you see your mother crying when your uncle, your father's brother, took you away and brought you to Jorum's home.

"Chenjerai, my friend, life is different for everyone." You pause briefly searching for the right words with which you want to tell her the story of your predicament. You want to tell her the truth but you falter on that because you are not so sure of Chenjerai's heart. Instead, tears of pain well up in your eyes. You look away so that she will not see them.

"Now, what is that supposed to mean, my friend? I think I know what makes you cry. Perhaps your family has perished because of this big disease with a small name. You are not the only one whose parents have been taken away by this disease." Chenjerai comes over and wipes away your tears with Muchaneta's towel. What she is doing should be done by your mother, you think to yourself. You wish you were home with her.

"Look at me my friend. I'm younger than you, but do you see what the disease has done to me already? It took away my husband and it will take me or my daughter any time." You sniff twice and then carry on. "My Muchaneta is shrivelling and wasting away like a mushroom in the sun. She has lost appetite. She cries all day long and is only quiet when she sleeps like this."

"That's why I've suggested that you should go and seek your mother's wisdom concerning your baby's and your own well-being."

86

Suddenly you hear voices in your head. They seem to be the same voices that talked to you before your uncles went to consult a *n'anga* back home. The voices are so loud that you wonder whether Chenjerai is not hearing them too. Then they seem to be the voices of your ancestors. They are accusing you of abandoning them. They are arguing amongst themselves, but you are not sure what their argument is about. You are afraid but you do not know what you are afraid of.

Muchaneta wakes and starts to cry for her milk. The voices fade into the baby's cries. You sit up and bring out the thin breast and put it into her already sucking mouth.

"I'll see you tomorrow then. I must go fetch water now." Chenjerai stands up collecting her skirts carefully and tying her *zambia* around her waist. You want to persuade her to stay a little bit longer but you do not have the will to do so. The words remain unuttered on your tongue.

\*

Today the wind is blowing from the north-west. It is light and fresh although hot. It registers its presence by shaking the tender leaves of the *musasa* and *munhondo* trees. The cicadas are clinging to the branches of these trees and are busy piping their incessant songs. A kite circles the mountain top. Perhaps up there it has built its nest among the bare boulders.

Chenjerai's idea is floating in your mind like what the kite is doing in the heated air above the mountain. All night you have been considering it over and over trying to decide what to do. You are undecided over two things. The first one is to go back to your home. The second is to write a letter to your mother. The first option is quite impossible. The cost of bus fare is very high. It is quite difficult for you to raise twenty million dollars for a to and fro journey to your homeland. The other reason is that you cannot go back to your mother. Your father and your uncles would not allow that. It had been agreed that I'm not to return home until the *ngozi* had stopped killing your uncles. So, it is the second option that you find possible. For about sixty thousand dollars, a letter is the cheapest way to communicate with your mother.

Now the pen is in your right hand poised over the blank exercise book page on which you intend to put words and send them to your mother. You are not sure how you can begin this letter. The pen remains in the air for a minute or two. Perhaps this is because of the long time that has gone by without writing to the people you left back home. Suddenly the flood of words that had seemed to rush into your mind has dried up. You are really trying to trap them again and confine them to the white paper before you. Words are strange things. They crowd your mind when pen and paper are not nearby, but are hard to find when they are most needed like now when pen and paper are there. But you are determined to write the letter. You are going to trap them along the blue lines of the white paper whether they like it or not. So, you begin:

Dear Mother,

The aches of my heart and the burdens of my life have forced me to write this letter. I don't know how long it is going to be, but judging from the time we have been apart expect this letter to be a very long one.

To begin with I want to tell you that despite not writing you, you still remain in my mind whenever I am not occupied with the problems that I am dipped in. The family that I joined took me in not as a child but as a daughter-in-law, the wife of their son. As soon as I arrived here, the village elders decided that I should be taken to the city where my husband-to-be was working. He was as old as my father. Although he was that old, he had no wife and no children that I have heard of. They say that he has lost three wives. Rumours tell me that they all died of the big disease. His mother has not revealed this to me. When I heard this, I became very afraid and worried. Unfortunately, I heard this after I had lived long enough to have a baby with him. Now I am afraid that Jorum has infected me with the disease and that is affecting me mentally.

Mother, I regret that you brought me into this world as a female person. Had I been in the image of my father, this story would not have been told. I would not have been the compensation price for a crime committed by my grandfather. I would not have been forced to be wife to Jorum. I would not have been infected by the seeds of death that I think course through my veins today. Is it a crime to be born a girl or a woman who can be used to pay for crimes?

Mother, you should be here to see your granddaughter Muchaneta. She is now ten months old but looks six. When I gave birth to her, she was a bouncing baby weighing two and a half kilos, but recently she has started wasting away. Maybe the seeds of death are also sprouting and growing in her blood now. How I wish you were here with me helping to look after her. She does not have enough food to eat and since the death of Jorum I have become the breadwinner in this home. My mother-in-law cares very little about me and the baby. She is always out at beer parties. She accuses me of having caused the death of Jorum. The people here do not believe the big disease is there therefore they have labelled me a witch. Think of it, mother! Your daughter is being called a witch.

I do not know what my supper is going to be tonight. My vegetable garden is dead because the dam has dried up. These are the moments when I always wish you were around. Do you know, mother, that if I were with you right now I would not have been a mother? Any way ...

"*Mai* Mucha, where are you?" The voice of your mother-in-law breaks the afternoon peace. You quickly hide the letter and pen in your skirts. Jorum's mother has warned you before against communicating with your people. She does not want you to do so. Maybe she thinks you are thinking of going back to your people.

"Over here, *amai*!" You reply at the same time smothering your clothes to conceal the letter. Your mother-in-law approaches you from her bedroom hut. One look at her and you know what she is up to. You are so used to her. It does not surprise you when she announces that she is on her way to the foot of the mountain where there was another beer party.

"What are we cooking for supper tonight?"

"Anything you can get your hands on," she replies knocking her snuff box on the heel of her palm. "My chickens are almost finished now, *muroora*."

The old lady follows the setting sun. You are left in the company of your haunting thoughts and your sickly daughter. The thoughts that cloud your mind are so deep and not for your age. They make you forget finishing the letter that you have been writing to your mother. In your mind you are hearing voices. They are the very voices that were coming to you when you were talking to Chenjerai the other day. You try several times to drive them away from your little head, but like bees at their hive, they fly around and hum making it difficult to drive them away all the more.

First Voice: *Break the silence. Tell the world what your fathers have done to you. Tell the world that what they have done to you is not different from what happened hundreds of years ago when our forefathers sold each other to the white man as slaves. Make humanity see sense.*

Second Voice: *Don't listen to that, young woman! What you're condemning is tradition handed down from generation to generation. You are too young to make ripples on this pool, no, not when you still have milk on your nose. Whatever you do will not change anything. Sew your mouth and stop whining over that.*

First Voice: *What tradition is it that makes the young and innocent people suffer? What tradition is it that kills the young to appease the long dead? What tradition is it that pays a debt of a cow with a goat? So, young woman break the silence and tell the world about these injustices on fellow women in your society. Go ahead. Question this tradition.*

Second Voice: *Be careful daughter of man! Don't insult your ancestor's ways by questioning what has been all this time.*

You are now confused. The voices wrestling in your young mind do not mind the turmoil that they are causing in you. They do not even mind that your mind is still so young to manage what the voices are arguing about. They are abusing your young mind. The subject of their wrangle can only be suitable for the ancestors. After a long time, they die down and peace returns to you.

# Chapter 9: Deformed Dreams

For a whole week now, you have been all over everywhere in the big city chasing after one of the two million phantom jobs that your president promised in the last elections. You had voted for him hopefully because you were dreaming of a good job after university especially after your widowed mother had literally closed her livestock pens in order for you to get the BSc degree that hangs proudly on the wall in your mother's sitting room. You had believed him without doubt that things were going to be on the mend and the economy would flourish birthing the jobs that would, perhaps, help to reopen the livestock pens of your mother. Disappointingly, three years into the five-year term of the old president, no jobs have been created for the millions of youths who are leaving school. Your anger and frustration boils inside you like a tropical volcano which would erupt any time as you trudge the potholed streets of the capital city.

On Monday, you had been to the light industry, just across the heavily polluted river, where you had heard over the weekend that a Chinese company was recruiting people to pack plastic toys that they were manufacturing. For four hours, you had waited outside the gate amongst the growing number of job-seekers only to be told by this fat, balding Chinese man that they wanted those with a BSc degree for the ten vacancies that were available. And you had forgotten your degree certificate at home. So, you were just like the others who had no education at all. You slouched away like a hyena whose kill has been taken over by a very hungry pride of lions.

Then on Tuesday you woke up before the sun showed above the eastern horizon and arrived at the site where the American

Embassy was constructing its new headquarters in the city. The contracted company wanted 'daga-boys' and you had remembered to take with you your BSc degree certificate just in case they wanted degreed 'daga-boys'. To your disappointment, the interview required that an applicant should be able to throw a brick high up to the second floor of the building. Your efforts, unfortunately, could not send a standard brick further than the first floor. It was a very disgraceful day especially when other young men like you could do with ease what you had failed to do.

Wednesday: another unfortunate day. A fertilizer company in the heavy industrial area wanted people to off-load a whole train that had hurled two hundred tonnes of fertilizer from the seaport into the country. These were 50kg net bags and you are only 47kg with your clothes and shoes on.

"You'll be paid according to the number of bags you will off-load," the foreman announced as soon as you were engaged. "This means you'll stack your bags in one stack and at the end of the day we'll count them. The more you off-load the more you earn. It's 50cents a bag."

No one was turned away. It was half past seven in the morning. There were men and women who had answered to the call for the job. The fifty-odd of you who had gathered for the job earnestly attacked the train like ants attacking the carcass of a dead python. The employer had assigned his permanent workers to climb into the wagons so that they would load the bags onto your heads and you would then carry them into the warehouse. So, when the first 50kg bag of urea landed on your dread-locked head, your knees buckled under you and before the bag crushed you under, you let fall to the platform and its powdery contents were all over.

"You're fired, boy! This work for men," the foreman was fuming as he shooed you out of the warehouse yard.

And that was the end of your job. All the castles you had built came crumbling on you like the bag of urea.

The previous day, Thursday, you spent it in First Street playing street soccer with other university graduates. The WhatsApp group message had requested you to come dressed in your graduation gown complete with the mortar-board, hood and rolled up papers to represent the certificates. The occasion was meant to be a statement-making get together to protest the president's failure to create the 2.2million jobs promised in the run-up to the 2013 elections. In attendance, the message said, would be the riot police – per the vendors, it was not those who quell riots but those who facilitate it to happen - and those queueing for their money at the banking halls in First Street

So, you had cordoned off the area between HM Barbours and Ok Stores for the stadium. By eight o'clock, the place was bristling with the police in their egg-heads, brandishing glass shields and batons that quivered like the spines of agitated hedgehogs. The game was played and the media had a field day. The following day the police where blamed by the politicians for allowing you to denigrate the name of the president like that. Your story was the subject of a heated debate in the parliament between the ruling party and opposition party members of parliament.

Today is Friday. Some call it *Faraiday* – a day to be happy. It is the end of the week and people celebrate it in many ways possible. Those with extra money to spend go to the taverns and beerhalls to drown their financial problems with liquor and others go for *gochi-gochi* to kill their craving for grilled meat. These celebrations require financing. So, on Thursday evening when you heard about the grave digging jobs that had been created at Mbudzi Cemetery by an undertaking company, you were there before the sun licked the eastern horizon of the city.

"We want people who can dig at least three graves a day," the pot-bellied prospective employer bellows after several picks and shovels have been off-loaded from the white truck that immediately drives off.

There is a scramble for the tools. In this disorganised melee you manage to grab a pick and a shovel. The rule here, as you learnt later, is that those who have not been able to lay their hands on a tool have not been hired. You are happy to have secured a pick and a shovel. Those who would have managed a pick or a shovel only have to work together and that meant splitting the pay at the end of the day. While waiting for the truck to arrive word had circulated saying that the employer only paid those who would have dug three graves per day. That way he was assured of finished graves since it was weekend, a time when most burials in the city were conducted.

Mr Pot Belly shows you where your work starts and ends. Soon sods of newly dug, sweet smelling soil are flying out and forming small hills next to the deepening rectangular holes you are digging.

Diggers are getting shorter and shorter as the holes deepen. Shirts have been taken off and are flapping on the handles of the picks or the shovels depending on which tool is in use at any given time. The whole area looks like a sweet potato field where moles are busy burrowing and creating mounds of soil everywhere. This is work for a man and a half and not for those who attended school at St George's or Peter House.

By the time you are waist deep callouses have popped up in your hands; your back is aching and your throat is as dry as a desert; you cannot swallow any saliva because there is none to swallow. When you stop to take a rest, a lot of thoughts flash through your mind. You remember when you were at St George's doing your fourth-year secondary school. You were a brilliant and eloquent student to the extent that your English language teacher had drafted you into the debate club which was mainly an Upper 6 elite club. You were so good at presenting your argument such that you became the opening speaker all the time you went for a debating competition. When you were in the Lower 6 you went overseas where you became the darling of audiences by beating the native speakers of the language. But then that was before your father's empire crumbled and he later died of stress resulting in your mother as well as you going to live in the rural areas. That was then and now after university you are facing the reality of your run-down country.

As the sun creeps to the zenith, you have not finished digging the first grave. Some of your fellow diggers are doing their second hole and others are starting on their third. Your hands are on fire. You dig for three minutes and take a rest of five. It would seem like you are not going to finish this one grave. The pain in your hands is very unbearable. You cannot bend your fingers to hold the handle of the pick anymore. But I'm an educated man, why should I suffer this way just like those who have not been to school, you ask yourself. Then what is the purpose of going to school if one has to do the work that an uneducated person can do? Who should answer that? You shake your head slowly as you contemplate whether to carry on working or quit at that moment.

The urge to quit overruns the one to keep digging. So, without telling Mr Pot Belly or anyone for that matter, you scramble out of the grave and you put on your shirt and head towards your aunt's house in the western part of the city. Two syllable words are spewing from your mouth as you walk away from the cemetery. You are cursing the day you were born: you are cursing the president of the country accusing him of blatant lying; you are so frustrated that you kick the stones out of your way. You blame the ruling party which created the situation that caused your father's companies to go under. You are so angry that you do not notice the shiny piece of metal that is revealed when you kick a stone out of your way until you are three strides away. Something tells you to go back and check what it is that is shining like that.

It is a folded $1 bond coin!

You pick up the deformed coin and brush off the little sand that clings to it. What could have made this coin to be folded like that, you wonder silently? You look at it carefully. No crack on it, right. Now many other things are crowding your muddled mind. It is Friday. A day when people celebrate the end of the week. At least I've somewhere to start from, you say to yourself as you quicken your steps towards the nearest bar. A $1 bond coin can buy you four litres of opaque beer. You are now feeling like a human being. Your gaiety is that of someone who has command of his destiny. The power of money! Isn't it the reason why people wake up early each day and run away from their warm and comfortable beds to look for, you muse as you enter the beerhall.

The noise in the beerhall does not reduce you to a beggar begging for *masese* from those who have the money to buy it. With exaggerated confidence, you walk straight to the barman.

"Barman, a two-litre pack of Super, please!" you proffer the folded $1 bond coin. You throat is already pumping like that of an angry frog.

The barman takes the deformed coin and looks at it.

"Sorry, we don't accept that kind of money." He literally throws it at you.

"But it's money, isn't it?"

"Not in this bar," the barman says as he goes to serve the next waiting customer.

All hope is gone. You pick up the deformed coin and go to sit at a table right in the darkest corner of the beerhall. You are afraid that he might think of calling the police and having you arrested for trying to defraud the beerhall. Alone in that dark corner, you listen to your hands throbbing and your back crack-aching and thinking: had the barman allowed you to buy with that deformed coin you would be wetting your throat with the thick Super which many people had christened: food and drink.

Then an idea dawns in your mind. You jump to your feet and quickly get out of the beerhall. Your legs take you towards the shops and surely there under the veranda, surrounded by boxes and boxes full of old broken shoes is the cobbler. He is busy applying glue to the sole of a shoe that he is repairing. The smell of glue is thick in the air around him.

"Excuse me, sir!"

The man looks up and then back at his handwork. "What is it, my son?"

"Can I use your hammer?"

"For what?"

You put your hand in your back pocket searching for the folded $1 bond coin. It is not there in that pocket. You check in the other and your hand comes out with it.

"I want to straighten this. The barman wouldn't take it like this."

The man continues applying glue to the sole of the shoe and you can see he has agreed to helping you. Then when he finishes what he is doing he stretches out his hand and you hand him the coin. He takes out his hammer and the cobbler anvil on which he puts the deformed coin. With two well directed strokes the coin is as good as new.

"Thank you very much," you say as you stretch your hand to receive the mended coin.

"Not before you have paid me." His whiskers are twitching like those of a cat that is preparing to eat a mouse it has just killed.

"How much?" you are calculating that if need be you will give him fifty cents and then you take the remainder to the barman and get yourself at least two litres of Super.

"One dollar fifty."

"Just for what you've done?"

"My charges start from one dollar fifty for any job that I do here, my son! So, you owe me fifty cents already if I keep this one."

You turn on your heels and walk away - dejectedly. When you turn around you see the cobbler caressing his *goatie* and a wicked smile crossing his lips.

# Chapter 10: As the Sun Threatens to Rise

Your story cannot be a story without the story of your grandfather having been told first. This is because your story is born from the story of your grandfather. Everything started in the summer of 1948. Kondo, your grandfather, was working on a farm belonging to Mr Smith. It was not by choice that he was working there, but it was by force – the silent force from the white masters who had come with their new rules and new ways of life. The settlers introduced forced labour in order to harness the black people to work for them for free. The circumstances surrounding forced labour are difficult for me to understand and explain. I still need to be filled in on that.

What I heard from my late grandfather is that when this white man was allocated that farm, your grandfather's clan had been living there for over four generations. This is what he told me when I visited him one day.

"On this land we had never known that a person can say this is my land." My great-grandfather said as he rolled tobacco on a piece of newspaper.

"So, who owned the land?" I asked the old man.

"The land belonged to no one and to everyone. Anyone could use it to graze his cattle, grow crops or hunt and would leave it for the next generation. It was a priceless heritage."

"Land was never sold or bought?"

"That's true," the old man said. "Land was neither bought nor sold. It was these people without knees who brought this unheard-of idea that has puzzled and troubled us all these years. Let me tell you that when Mr Smith came to take up the farm he evicted the people and grabbed their cattle, goats and sheep. He had bought it and therefore it was his. He was helped by the police to do this. Kondo's people were driven to the valley north of this country. This valley is very hot throughout the year; it is drought stricken all the time and tsetse-fly and mosquito infested. This did not stop the white settlers from demanding hut tax from Kondo and his people. Those who understand this very well say that taking the people's land and asking them to pay tax were the white man's ways of bringing the black people to use money. So, the need for tax money drove Kondo back to Mr Smith's farm to look for work so that he could be able to pay the hut tax that the new settler government demanded from him. He had to leave his wife, your grandmother, looking after your father and his siblings."

It was from this conversation with your grandfather that I learnt about what was happening during those early days of this country. I have also heard it said that life on the farms was not really good, but one could get used to it if one lived there long enough.

One day while planting Mr Smith's tobacco, a messenger came to the field where your grandfather was working with the others. Zhuwaki, the foreman, gathered the workers together before making the following announcement:

"The *baas* wants a 'shoot-boy'. His maize crop is about to mature and therefore he doesn't want it destroyed by the wild pigs like what happened last year. He has asked me to choose a person for that job."

"What's that?" One of the workers asked Zhuwaki.

"It's a job where one goes around shooting the wild pigs that would be destroying maize in the fields."

"So?" Kondo asked as he looked around with apprehension. Zhuwaki looked at the workers as if waiting for them to scramble for this new job that was on offer but no one came forward to claim it. Eventually his eyes stopped on your grandfather.

"I'm choosing you for the job."

"Who?" He pointed at himself with his tobacco stained forefinger. "Me?"

"Yes, you. You'll stop doing what you are doing right away. You must leave your small hoe and go to see the *baas* in his office. You will work with a rifle now."

Kondo was further taken aback by this appointment. He had not expected the foreman to choose him of all people gathered there.

Later that change of work meant a lot of things to Kondo. It meant less gruelling work, meat for his pot and time to drink *kachasu,* the portent brew distilled illegally in the compound. Your grandfather, I was to know later, liked hunting with dogs before the clan was relocated to the valley. So, he gladly accepted the offer. It reminded him of the days he used to hunt small game on the very same land with four or five dogs before the arrival of the white man. He knew all the ravines and the overgrown anthills where the pigs hide during the day and the trails that they used at night as they went about foraging for food.

Mr Smith drove him to the firing range at the police camp and gave him a few lessons on how to handle the shotgun he was going to use. He learnt how to strip and clean the rifle, target shooting and the discipline attached to the use of fire arms. The new job excused him from the hard field work that had bent his back like an overstrung bow. No more was he going to toil in the sun and rain. He really hated *mugwazo* where they were given piece-work on Saturdays and would dismiss when they finished weeding the allocated portion. Now Kondo had become his own boss and worked at his own pace and time reporting directly to the white man only. He went out at night and spent the whole day sleeping in his house. He was off every Saturday and Sunday. There was no job like the one that he had landed.

It was on such a Sunday, the third in the month of January, that your story really started. Farm workers are lowly paid people. That is what I have been told and looking back and imagining the events of that fateful day, I can see why they say that. The little money that they got from the white man could not last throughout the month. Because of that, farm workers were referred to as the BSAP, not the British South African Police, but this meant people who went 'broke soon after pay'. It was this little pay that drove them to excessive drinking to the extent that they did not mind being three or four times their pay indebted to those who sold the beer on the farm.

Working on farms had its own form of corruption, they say. Those who had positions of power had ways of benefiting from those positions. Therefore, the foreman who had chosen Kondo to be a 'shoot-boy' expected something in return. One evening, at a *kachasu* party, the following conversation took place between Zhuwaki and your grandfather.

"My friend, don't forget that it is I, Zhuwaki, the foreman, who got you that job in the first place. You should definitely *remember* me. If it wasn't for me your back would by now have become a bow"

"I know that, but how many times should I be doing this? Did I not bring you a whole wild pig to thank you for that promotion?" Kondo was now drunk but he kept the *kachasu* bottle in his hand.

"Do you want to lose that job tomorrow? Do you want to go back to the field and join the others in the fields?"

"No, *vakuru vangu*," Kondo was pleading now. "What exactly are you saying?"

Zhuwaki looked slyly at him in the dim glow of the fire in the little hut they were sitting before saying: "That my children have not forgotten the taste of the last wild pig you gave me. And they are always asking me when another one is coming?"

"Only that," Kondo took a swig from his *bomba*. It attacked him and he contorted his face as if stung by a bee. It trickled down the gullet into his already boiling stomach. "I'll shoot one for you tomorrow morning, but there's one thing."

"Which is?" The foreman was smiling now. All the slyness had disappeared from his face. He had won again. He would win any other time. His power and influence were invincible.

"You'll collect it yourself. I will bring it near the dam around 4 a.m. I don't want to be seen again like we almost did last time."

"Who'll see you? Am I not second to the white man here? No one will ever find fault in that. What I say goes."

"No, no, no! Remember the instructions *murungu* gave to me."

"That all wild pigs you kill must be brought to the *baas*. I'm also a *baas* to you." The foreman thought for a moment and then said, "Four o'clock then at the dam."

Later in the night Kondo was seen staggering drunkenly towards the hut of his girlfriend. He was there a little while but sometime in the night two silhouettes were seen getting into Kondo's bedroom. It was just after midnight.

Your grandfather, as you know, was one person who was never overpowered by alcohol. At four o'clock in the morning he went out with his shot gun. It was a double barrel rifle, the kind that guinea-fowl hunters use. By this time of the year the maize was ripening. It was that time when wild pigs will be breeding. He skirted the maize field starting from the north. In the early morning light, he could not see far since there was no moon. Even if there was a moon it was not going to shine because the sky was over cast. It was threatening to rain that early morning.

He walked quietly, listening, trying to pick out the sound of snapping maize stalks among the myriad sounds of the night. He would walk some twenty paces, stop and listen, but it was quiet all over. Now and again a nightjar with those long wing feathers would club the air after he had disturbed it from its nocturnal rest. An easterly breeze disturbed the leaves of the crop producing swish-swashing sounds occasionally punctuated by the hoot of an owl now and again. Sometimes in his drunken plod he heard the sound that he was listening for but all the time it proved to be false as it turned out that it was all in his imagination. Besides the rustling of the maize leaves, it was indeed a quiet night by comparison – a night fit for shooting pigs.

The maize field dipped towards the dam which was on the stream that cut the farm into two. When Kondo reached the near-end of the field, he followed its width and upon reaching the width-end, he turned and traced the length side of the field, away from the dam. By now the *drongos* were calling, heralding the approach of dawn. If it was not overcast, by now twilight could have tinted the eastern horizon. Still Kondo had not heard a pig foraging in the maize field. He was beginning to fear for his job now. Zhuwaki was one of those foremen who could influence the decisions of the white men they worked for. A word of discontentment spoken to the *baas* about a worker could result in that worker being fired. If he could not shoot a pig that morning how was he going to explain that to the foreman? In the same breath it was not his fault that there were no pigs to kill that morning. It would not be his lucky day. Days are not the same, he told himself. He hoped that Zhuwaki would understand that.

As he was going past the outcrop of rock that they used to sit when taking tea-breaks every time they worked in that field he heard the rustling of maize leaves. This was the sound that he had tuned his ears to hear. Kondo stopped. He cocked the shotgun. He listened again.

*

The sky was not clear. No stars could be seen up there. It was dark outside, so dark that he could not even see the kitchen hut from the front of the house where he stood yawning. By the second cock crow the foreman was up. A warm moist wind breezed from the east rustling the gum tree leaves that towered above his house. With it came the smell of wet mud from the river and the croaking voices of tired frogs. *Whoo! Whoo!* An owl hooted from the top of that tree. Another replied from the *muvanga* tree in the middle of the field that bordered the compound. *Drongos* could be heard calling in the forest to the west of Mr Smith's compound. Like Kondo, the *kachasu* that he had been drinking the previous night was still in his breath. A lingering dizziness almost persuaded him not to go to meet the 'shoot-boy'. Zhuwaki stood for a while. It was as if he was waiting for his eyes to adjust to the darkness. He had slipped out of bed without his wife stirring. She was a sound sleeper.

After the second yawn he walked towards the kitchen hut and went in. He was in there, dark as it was, for a while. Eventually he came out carrying a wheelbarrow. He was careful not to bang it against the door or the door frame. Quietly he closed the wooden door and hoisted the wheelbarrow onto his head. This made him look like a man wearing a big hat with two prongs jutting out to the back. Because his house was a distance from the rest of the compound and that it was night time he managed to depart without anyone seeing him. It was not going to be good for him to be spotted carrying the wheelbarrow instead of pushing it. Anyone who would see him like that at that unholy hour would be suspicious. But, pushing the empty wheelbarrow was going to make it make noise resulting in people hearing his movements. Although he was the most powerful black person on the farm, there were some things that needed secrecy – like fetching a boar from the fields at that time of the day. Nevertheless, the foreman needed to go and collect the wild pig that Kondo had promised him. He wanted to come back quickly and prepare it before he went to work at seven. His wife and children would be very happy cleaning and cutting it up for the pot. He was a man who liked to pleasantly present his family with a surprise.

His legs were still unsteady from the bingeing he had taken part in, but he managed to carry the empty wheelbarrow quietly, through the forest of the calling *drongos*, up the tractor road that snaked its way between the small hills that were like the budding breasts of a young girl, then he dipped towards the river only to cross it over the earth dam wall a while later. In twenty minutes', time he had reached the dam. He proceeded to the agreed rendezvous. By now the easterly wind had become a little warmer and was wafting down the river valley and, in its wake, mist began to follow, forming a wispy whitish line that traced the river valley. His eyes had become used to the darkness by now.

Time passes slowly when you are waiting for something to happen. A minute is like an hour, a day is like a week. It is a time of brooding, a time when thoughts haunting as well as pleasing ferment inside the mind of a waiting man. Zhuwaki was not an exception to this. His mind created possibilities and failures as he sat on the rock. What if Kondo had over slept and had not even come out to hunt the pigs? He was so drunk yesterday I remember his voice was slurry. I should have checked him at his house before coming down here. Kondo could have changed his mind and decided not to go out for me. Had he not refused to shoot another pig for me yesterday before I threatened him with taking the job from him? I don't trust anyone who begins by refusing what I will have suggested. That's where I'm different from all the other black people on the farm. At least I'm honest and the white man trusts me because of that. I'm very time conscious in whatever I do.

Zhuwaki waited for about half an hour before he decided to get into the maize crop to await Kondo. The wind was nippy where he was waiting. He sat down on an outcrop of rock that had prevented planting a few rows into the maize field. This was the same place where workers took their tea break when working in that section of the farm. The foreman was sure that he was going to hear Kondo's gumshoes when he came along. After a long wait, Zhuwaki heard the plop-plopping of Kondo's wet wellingtons. There was no one else who could move in those areas during that time of the day. He knew that it was him but when he listened more carefully, he realised that he was not coming to the clearing. This made the foreman think that perhaps there was a misunderstanding about where they were supposed to meet. Therefore, when Kondo had gone five or six paces past the place he was sitting, the foreman stood up and rushed towards him to let him know that he was waiting there. In his quick movement he crushed through the maize crop breaking some of it, making the noise that the hunter had been listening for all along. The foreman only saw the fire as he rushed to accost Kondo. He did not hear the roar of the shot-gun. The pellets took him full in the stomach. Zhuwaki groaned before he died.

Kondo heard the groan of the dying man and thought that he had shot and killed his quarry. From his belt he took out his long hunting knife. He entered the maize crop quickly intending to cut the throat of the dead animal so that it can bleed, but he was shocked by what he wanted to collect. Instead of the wild pig, he had shot and killed a man! He switched on his hunting torch, and there lying like a drunken man was Zhuwaki, the foreman, lifeless. This discovery shocked him so much that he took to his heels for a short distance before his head started to work rationally. He came back where Zhuwaki was. Sweat beads started to form all over his brow. His stomach heaved and he nearly threw up from the smell of the foreman's entrails. He could feel the warmth from his body wafting to his face. It was after a long time that he steadied himself and came back to the foreman's body. He sat on the rock outcrop for a long time trying to think until he realised that he had to do something quickly. Morning was approaching and he did not want to regret his procrastination.

His mind started running around. Was this the meaning of his promotion to become a 'shoot-boy'? How was he going to report this to the white man? Would Mr Smith believe him? What about the foreman's wife? What was she going to say about the death of her husband? The answers to all these questions were not there.

The only thing that crept in his mind was the looming prison or death by hanging. His imagination ran wild. There were many people he knew who had been to jail who had come back telling horrifying stories of the life inside. Sodomy, hunger, beatings by the wardens, brutal fights and hard labour, he had heard, were rife in the prisons of the country. He pictured himself going through all these nasty prison things. A cold shiver ran through his body for the umpteenth time. Although it was early in the morning more sweat beads continued to form on his face. The big ones rolled down his face dropping to be swallowed by the cloth of his clothes.

In the next quarter of an hour the mist thinned out and cleared. By now the sun was threatening to rise and chase the darkness of the night away. Dark clouds started scudding from the east covering the whole sky like thick black cotton fluffs. It looked like it was going to rain at that early hour. Looking around from where he sat Kondo's eyes fell on the wheelbarrow and an idea flushed into his mind. This was it, he told himself as he heaved himself up to lift the foreman's body. He was careful not to have blood soaking into his clothes. He put the body in the wheelbarrow. It was easier to carry the body that way. From the paddock nearby, he broke off a piece of wire long enough for his intentions. Kondo tied one end of the wire around the dead man's neck leaving a longer piece. This piece he then tied to the wheel of the wheelbarrow. Then he loaded the dead body into the wheelbarrow.

A short while later a single loud splash was heard at the deep end of the lake. At that moment, as if by conjures, it started to rain heavily. The big drops sounded on the maize crop like a shower. Kondo was relieved that the rain was going to obliterate any tell-tale of the death of the foreman. The cold rain washed away the little blood that had soaked into his overall too. Kondo heaved a big sigh of relief and picked up his shot-gun.

# Chapter 11: The Big Noise

We heard the big noise with our little ears. It was a strange noise. We had never heard a noise that loud except in summer when clouds rose up into the sky, and in them and under them jagged bolts of lightning preceded the empty drum-like rumbling that sent me hiding between Mother's bags of groundnuts behind the door in her kitchen hut. Everyone in my family knew that thunder and lightning were my worst enemies. If a thunderstorm developed and they were about to eat deliciously prepared chicken, I wasn't going to be part of that. And now, coming from some unknown place, the big noise shook the ground and echoed from the hills on the other side of our beautiful valley. The chickens scurried to hide under the granary while the birds flew from the trees and landed on the rooftops of our huts – something that they had never done before, considering the fact that we trapped them, shot them and stole their young as well as eggs. Normally they keep their distance so as not to be hit by the stones we threw. But today the confused birds tweeted loudly and almost flew into the huts where we kept the pots in which we would cook them.

The village was often quiet in the hot summer afternoon, but on this day, the mighty sound disturbed the peace and increased in volume as if it was drawing closer. We felt it inside our bodies; it rattled our chests and rocked our feet. We searched this way and that way; upwards and downwards but nothing appeared on the horizon. We looked silent and fearful questions at each other. It was just too complicated for two little boys like us to understand. We wished our parents were there to explain to us what was happening. All this time our hearts thumped like mortars being worked by over-aged girls who had lost glorious opportunities to get married.

We looked around for suitable hiding places, perhaps under the granary where the chickens had taken refuge? But what if the thing that was making the huge noise was much larger than our granary? Wouldn't we be flattened under it? I imagined dying under the granary together with our chickens and perhaps all the rats in the homestead. We looked at the big *mukuyu* tree that stood in the middle of the homestead. Would we be safe up there from where the birds had flown away? Maybe the birds, because they were always up above us, had seen the thing whose noise had drowned every other sound in the village. And if so, the thing would not find it difficult to pluck us from that tree just like ripe figs ready for the mouth. We looked at the lush bush that surrounded our home, but those were only bushes; they were not thick enough to make us invisible. Moreover, if the thing were tall, then it was not a good idea to seek a hiding place there. We looked at the river – our big river. It ran just a spitting distance from the village. Our minds discarded that idea because a week before one of our calves had been dragged into the water by a crocodile. Father only found its head stashed in the caves on the opposite bank the following day. Our grandfather, the father of my father, had recently told us to keep our shadows away from the waters of this mighty river lest a crocodile drag us in by our shadows. And which one of us would like to die between the yellow teeth of that monster?

The most unfortunate thing was that we were all alone at home. Our parents and older siblings had gone to the fields for the second shift of the day's weeding. We had been left 'looking' after the home. The two of us were supposed to play guard, but the booming sound that was creeping upon us had reduced us to cowards rather than the warriors of valour that we were meant to be. But the noise grew louder by the minute. When I looked at my brother, who was a year older than me, I saw fear stamped all over his face. But what really shocked me was the river of yellowish liquid that streamed down his shins to his bare feet. His bladder must have given in and surrendered to the fear-inducing sound that we had never heard in our valley.

'Let's follow the elders to the fields,' I suggested in between the chattering of my teeth.

'Nonsense! That's where the thing making the noise is coming from. You don't want to walk yourself into its mouth.' My brother quickly nullified my 'good' idea.

'You're right.' I felt my foolishness mix with the fear of the approaching unknown demons. 'That thing must be huge and the mouth that gives out such a huge noise must be huge too. We will be eaten alive.'

We wondered why our parents had not run back home from the fields. Had the approaching monster eaten them already? If our parents had been eaten who were we to survive the threat of death that had taken our parents and older siblings? These questions made me feel helpless and it was then I felt the hot yellow liquid coursing down my grey shins too. My brother looked at me but saw nothing funny in this.

Then, as we pondered what to do, where to hide and when to do what we had to do, we both looked where the horrendous noise was coming from, and there, just above the tree tops we saw plumes of black smoke shooting into the afternoon air. Our imaginations ran wild.

'Could it be a big fire coming to roast us alive?' I asked my brother.

'I don't want to know.' Like me he was shivering as if he had just finished having a forced cold bath in winter.

*Sekuru*, our mother's brother, the one who came home at the end of the year with packets of sweet things and bread and jam and clothes for us, once told us about a place high above the clouds where bad people were roasted on a fire that did not die down.

That was a story then.

'Do you remember?' I asked my brother.

'I don't want to remember, please!' My brother was almost crying.

We scarpered behind the granary just to avoid seeing the approaching black smoke and whatever was making it. A giant rat suddenly came scrambling from the eaves of the roof to fall right at our feet. We screamed as we jumped backwards simultaneously. The rat scampered under the granary and we ran back where we had come from.

Meanwhile the huge noise, by now, was almost upon us but still, because of the thick bush, we could not see what was causing it. The smoke was now drifting towards us. It smelt like Father's sandals when an ember of burning wood fell on one of them. Judging from the different pitches of the deep-throated growls we were now quite sure that it was not one thing but several of them approaching our home. We scurried around like confused ants whose nest has been unintentionally trampled by a cow. The home, our home, had become a place of insecurity.

Then the first one appeared.

It was bigger than the elephants that visited our maize racks at night to rob us of our year's pumpkin and maize harvest. They were *nhundurwa* in colour and had large hand-like extensions that looked like the back legs of a grasshopper. These supported a huge knife-like scoop that looked like it had cut through a lot of things in its life. Under it we could see chain-like things which plodded ahead like the feet of a very large elephant, one at a time like a fast-

114

moving snail. Above it was a big black pipe that belched out the black plumes of smoke that we had seen above the treeline. The monster crushed trees that were on its path like grass after a heavy storm. It was such a mesmerising creature that we froze on the spot for a short while. Though filled with fear, I admired the power and the unstoppable desire of the thing to destroy anything in its path.

We did not wait to see the others stop just outside our home. We dashed to the back of our mother's kitchen hut where the granary stood. I slid under and pushed to one side where the chickens that had also taken refuge there were. My chest was almost bursting with fear and my mouth was dry. I could feel the warm liquid wetting my 10oz. shorts again where I lay with my face buried in the dusty ground under the granary.

The loud noises had now subsided to a quiet drone similar to that produced by the black wasps that often built their nests in the conical roof of Mother's cooking hut. Then we heard voices. Some of them I could not identify but I heard Father's voice distinctly. It was not his usual one. It seemed he was not happy. Some of what the other people were saying did not make sense to us. I looked in the direction from where the voices came. I saw Father's feet – I couldn't mistake those tyre sandals that he had been wearing since time immemorial – and another pair in black boots that shone like the outside of Mother's cooking clay pots.

'The *bwana* says a big dam is going to be built here whether you like it or not,' someone who spoke our language said.

'Ask your *bwana* whether we were ever informed of that. How can government do that to us? Are we not citizens of this country?' Father asked. His feet shifted the way they always did when he was angry. I could clearly imagine his facial expression as he asked these questions. From under the granary I could not tell how the people he was talking to looked. I watched more pairs of feet lifting up and down as their owners walked about our yard.

Then I saw Mother's cracked feet walking all over the place. They went to the *mukuyu* tree and then came back to the cooking hut. Sometimes they stopped. The feet went to my parents' sleeping hut and remained there for quite a while. Why was she moving around like that? Could she be looking for us? I, for one, was not going to come out and be devoured by those big monsters that were now droning and puffing at the edge of our home like tired hunting dogs after a long day of chasing rabbits.

'Chamunorwa! Munorwei!' I heard the thin voice of Mother call our names. I looked at Munorwei. He looked back at me. I now thought: if we come out of hiding, would those monsters eat us in the presence of our mother and father? Mother would not allow that. She loved us, her children, very much. She would fight for us as she did when our big sister had a problem with the boy from the home next door. I was much younger then, but I remember how Mother bit the mother of that boy with her big white teeth that turned red with the other woman's blood. The details of what had happened to provoke that fight are not clear to me even today.

'Chamu! Muno!' Mother called again. 'Now, where are those children?' she asked no one in particular.

As we watched, her feet came towards the granary. She opened the door and climbed inside. We heard her rummaging through the sacks of maize and *mhunga* that she kept there. Her feet could be heard thudding above us. Then they climbed down and we saw her knees and hands touching the ground. And finally, her face looked at us. We crawled out with our wet shorts covered in dust.

*

By mid-May we had finished gathering our crops from the fields. The date for our relocation was almost upon us. Our goats and donkeys were now free ranging in the fields, eating the remnants of the maize crop. We went about hunting mice and grasshoppers to supplement our food. The huge machines that had come two months earlier had already started work at the place where the mountains constricted the river valley. Every day we heard them groaning and bellowing there. We did not know what they were really doing, as we were never allowed to wander far from home. We heard that they had come to build a huge dam. As children, we were never told what that meant. The snippets of information that came our way were gleaned from the adults who always spoke in hushed tones about not wanting to be relocated far away from the land of their ancestors and from the graves of their forefathers.

We did not understand some of these things; they were too complicated for our simple little minds. We heard that the dam was going to be very useful to many people in that it would provide lots of water and fish. We did not see any sense in that because our river gave enough water for our winter crops and there were fish as big as myself that people caught. The adults also said that the dam was going to be used for generating electricity, which would benefit the country. Which country and what was that animal called electricity? We asked ourselves these questions when we were out chasing birds and grasshoppers in the valley. We did not know that there was something called a country at all. Our horizon and the hills that stood at the edge of the valley defined our life and our existence under the sun.

For more than a week, the men of the village gathered at my father's *dare* to exchange views in hushed voices about something that we could not understand. The only words that we heard and heard clearly were that we, the children, should never be allowed to hear what they were talking about because we had small hearts. Even our mothers were kept away from these discussions. But in the secrecy of their daily deliberations we heard words like *nyakanyaka*, *vana vevhu* and *vapambepfumi*. And when the men of the village said these words they were very angry and punched the air with their clenched fists, but we did not see anyone who they were angry at. Sometimes they ended the meeting by singing a song that we had never heard before. One late afternoon we sang the song while going to fetch the goats from the river and Father took a green stick and thrashed our dusty legs telling us never to sing that song again.

One night, I woke up suddenly. I thought I was dreaming, but I was not. In the darkness, I clearly heard someone calling Father's name. After three calls his sleeping hut door made its usual sound when someone opened it from inside. Then I heard his tyre-sandal clad feet crunching the gravel as he walked away from home. I wondered where he was going and who was calling him at that time of the night. I had heard that witches can call people if they want to ride them like horses to go and attend to their business. I tried to wake my brother but he was not one who was easily disturbed at night when he was sleeping. His snoring increased when I shook him and became even deeper, so I gave up and left him like that.

When the last *drongo* chirped on the *mukuyu* tree indicating that day was about to break, I heard the crunching gravel again. This time I got up on my elbows and peeped through the gap between the doorframe and the door to see Father walking towards the granary. He looked tired. On his shoulder was a shovel. This was strange to me. I tried to make sense of it but my mind fell short of solving the mystery of the shovel and the night disappearance. He threw the shovel under the granary before going into his sleeping

118

hut. He did not come out until midday when Mother went to give him food.

Two days, three days, four days went by quietly without incidence. On the fifth day, early in the morning, we were roused by loud banging on my parents' door. Night had not yet said goodbye to the valley but the east was ripening into day slowly. I looked through the crack to see two men standing at my parents' door. Father came out half-dressed. The two men immediately grabbed him and put his arms behind him. Why his arms remained there I could not understand because I knew Father as a very strong man who could carry heavy logs from the forest when Mother wanted to make beer. One of the men hit Father on the head with what looked like a thick stick and he swayed like a tree that was about to fall after being cut but he didn't hit the ground because the other man kicked him in the stomach and he came up straight. Mother came out screaming at the top of her voice. I scrambled out of my blankets and ran to the scene. That's when I heard screams from other homes in the village.

'How can you burn equipment belonging to the government?' one of the men said pushing Mother to the ground. 'We will teach you a lesson you will never forget before we throw you in jail. The dam project you want to stop has cost government a lot of money and you think you are more important than the project.'

'We will show you that government is more powerful than you.' Baton blows rained on Father as the man spoke. Who was this person called government who wanted to build a dam in our village? Why didn't that person build it somewhere else? These questions and many others troubled my small mind.

By now the sun was coming up over the eastern horizon. The men drove Father, kicking him and whacking him with the black batons, to where their leader, a white man, was waiting. More village men were herded there, all with their hands tied at the back. From where I stood with Mother I could see that these men, like Father, had been thoroughly beaten. Some had blood on their shirtfronts while others, men I knew not to have limps before, were limping like their legs had been broken. I did not understand why these strong men from my village, men who would kill an elephant or a lion with spears, did not fight back.

Before long, most of the men of our village had been forced to sit down in front of the white man. They looked defeated and dejected. From a distance, we heard the drone of a lorry climbing down the valley using the same way that was used by the big machines that our fathers were said to have burned, forcing their drivers to run away. It arrived in a flurry of dust and smoke. The men were loaded into it before being driven away to a place we did not know.

The following week a convoy of very green lorries arrived in the valley. Our mothers and brothers loaded some of our belongings into them. We were not allowed to take our goats with us because the lorries were full. We sat on top of our belongings and the lorries drove out of the valley slowly, swaying like drunken giants on the uneven road, as if giving us time to say goodbye to our ancestors' graves. As we topped the hills, we saw plumes of smoke going up to join the afternoon clouds.

'My children,' Mother said, wiping tears from her eyes, 'don't look back because you will never come back here again.'

# Chapter 12: The Other Side of the Cemetery

There were rows upon rows of headstones in this silent park. Lush green grass growing in-between the rows said a lot about the soil on which the grass was growing. Gwede had always cut the grass short and trimmed it at the edges the way some men did their hair and beard. He always made sure that the grass did not grow to ankle height. He always brought his petrol-driven lawn mower and left the air tingling with the fresh smell of cut grass. Those visitors who are susceptible to the smell of cut grass always sneezed and wheezed with their noses stuck in handkerchiefs. The weeping willows which were planted around the perimeter of this place swayed in the slightest breeze. Geraniums and the bougainvillea, used to form arches at the entrance, gave it a garden atmosphere.

A 1984 Toyota Custom Crown crawled like an old cockroach through the bougainvillea-arched gate squeaking and creaking. Behind it followed the latest Jeeps, Toyotas and Mazdas with their hazards blinking like fire flies at the beginning of a savannah summer. Their engines purred like well-fed cats. Gwede only noticed the convoy when it was just behind him. The rattling motor of the lawn mower drowned the purring, the squeaking and the creaking of the cortege. He stopped and straightened up before taking out a small face towel to wipe the sweat that had beaded on his brow. It was a hot January day. The lawn mower rattled less loudly now that it was not chewing grass.

The seven cars wound their way through the gleaming headstones until they stopped near an empty hole that Gwede had dug earlier that morning. A man in black swallow tails, white shirt and a matching black top-hat alighted from the hearse and went to open the back door of the Custom Crown. He took out a wreath and bunches of flowers and handed them to one who appeared to be his aide. Other occupants of the other cars came out buttoning their three-piece suits, while the ladies straightened their cashmere black dresses. Some flipped open Chinese fans and started to fan their heavily made-up faces. They hung on the hands of their partners as if their lives depended on that alone. Gwede watched all this from under one of the weeping willows where he had gone to hide from the sun.

Four men went to the back of the hearse and removed an emerald casket. From the way they leaned towards the box, the contents of it must have been a big human. They staggered and stumbled as they laid it on the rack. Gwede switched off the lawn mower motor in order to hear what was going to be said at this burial.

The first to speak was the priest. "Ladies and gentlemen, we are gathered here today to plant another flower in this garden of death …" On hearing these words Gwede's eyes went wide. Was this a new way of looking at the cemetery? If this was a garden, then he was the gardener perhaps. He knew that flowers were natural plants created to give joy to those who looked at them. As regards people, girls and women were the only ones whom he thought could be described as flowers. The younger girls would be the buds and the mature women the blooms at their prime while the old women were the withering flowers. Could men also be called flowers?

He scratched his head, swatted at a fly and walked to the other side of the cemetery. He would come afterwards to do what he always did after the burial.

# Chapter 13: Echoes in my ears

The early September sun has been hot as early as eight o'clock today, and it shouldn't be since we are only a month away from winter when mornings remain chilly till about midday. It shimmers and makes the green rubber hedge trees dance as if they are reflections in a pool whose waters are being disturbed by water beetles. Cicadas, with not yet developed voices, punctuate this atmosphere with short strident screeches that one can use to time one's breathing accurately. The air is smoky from the burning huts in the deserted village. High up where the smoke cannot be seen because the blue smoke is the same colour as the sky, kites are circling watching the burning huts below.

It is breakfast time for the soldiers who now, with their FN rifles leaning against the walls of this homestead whose huts they had not set on fire, their kit bag zips ripped apart revealing the cans of beef and the dog biscuits, sit around the small gas stoves on which sit mess cans of boiling water and frying corned meats. The smell of cooking food stirs the hunger in my stomach for I last ate the previous day in the afternoon. My stomach growled.

With my hands cuffed at the back, I am seated in the sun where they can see me in case I have ideas of wanting to run away. On my left eyelashes I can see caked blood from the beating that I have received when they found me hidden in the garden of agony earlier in the morning. I cannot remove the dried blood. There is throbbing pain on my head where one of the soldiers hit me with the butt of a rifle, I think that is where the dried blood came from.

As I roast in the sun, flies are landing there and feasting on me, I can only shake my head to drive them away. I lick my lips, the upper one is thick, a sharp pain points me to another injury there.

That was inflicted by a boot that had knocked me down from where I was kneeling begging for mercy when they were beating me.

These are young men of my age; black men like me who have chosen to join the war on the other side. I can see from the thickness of their beards that they came out of the classroom to the bush – call-up, it is called. These days a young man, black or white, could not enter into a training college without having served in the security forces for six months which, for my part, was the reason why after finishing school and having passed very well, could not enter into a college or technical institution to train for a trade. I felt it unjust to fight against my brothers and sisters who wanted the country to go the one man one vote way, something the white government was not ready to extend to the black people. Now with fire power in their hands I can see that they have an upper hand on me.

"Stand up!" This one is nudging me with a military tan polished boot.

I stand up.

"Come sit near me in the shade." He is speaking in Shona.

He has made some coffee. The smell of this beverage is killing me.

"Why are wasting your time supporting the terrorists? Don't you know you could die for nothing?" He looks at me as if he is talking to his young brother who has decided to get married before him. In my mind I'm saying: and you, what would you die for? But I'm not telling him this. The fact of the matter is that people like him were dying each day on the sides of the conflict.

124

"You seem an educated young man. How far have you gone with school?"

"Ordinary level." I tell him in a low voice, not wanting the rest of the soldier to hear that I was that educated.

"Where did you attend school?"

"St Philip's, Magwenya."

"Ah, what a coincidence. My girlfriend who is doing nursing at Harare Hospital was there also. When were you there?"

"'77."

"So, you must have been in the same class? Do you know a girl called Jane Madimu?"

"Yes. We set close together in class." I am warming up to this young man and so is he to me.

"She's such a nice girl. Very understanding." He is drinking from his cup; nibbling at the biscuit like someone who feels guilty eating in my presence.

"Yes, she's a good girl – eh, woman now."

My mind is whisked two years back when I was in secondary school. Then we led an independent life – independent in the sense that we were far from the control of our parents. I remembered that Jane, who always wanted to be close to me, was a petite girl graduating into a full-bodied woman. Because of the one dimple on her left cheek, she appeared to be two people in one, this, depending on which side you were looking at her from. I often read to her sex scenes from the Nick Carter novels which were my favourites and showed her pictures from the pornographic Scope magazine. I could tell when her blood was racing through her veins from her heart with the excitement of unexplored eroticism when she sucked her forefinger or when she would go tap-tapping the flow with her foot as if trying to hide what I knew she was going through. Everybody in the school, even the principal, boarding master including the teachers, thought she was my girlfriend. But that was not so.

"Yes, she's a good girl." I repeat more to myself than to this young soldier.

While I am busy chatting to this young soldier, I feel a stab on my back side, that kind of stab inflicted by boring eyes when someone, does not just look at you wanting to see you, but a look which is filled with hot hate. Thus, I knew someone is looking at me without me looking to see who is looking at me. Hesitantly, I turn my head and my eyes meet with muddy-looking eyes, eyes without emotion, eyes that were predatory like those of a crocodile – those eyes that make you want to turn into a snail and retreat into your shell for your own safety. His light complexioned face has been blackened so much that he looks like the rest of them. One glance is enough, but that glance stayed with me for many, many years of my life.

"Terrorist, come here." He orders when he realises that I have cringed from his domineering look which had injected me with fear the way a snake injects poison into a mouse it wants to swallow. I'm sitting cross-legged and with my hands behind my back and the tiredness that is in my body, it's a struggle for me to get to my feet

When, eventually I balance myself on my feet and my head is swirling around like a deformed vinyl record on a turntable, I shuffle to this camouflaged man whose eyes drilled holes into me.

He stands up, corks his rifle and points to the edge of the yard. From the stripes on his epaulettes he seems to be in charge of the troop.

"Run!" He barks at me.

I'm confused. Why should I run?

"Run, terrorist, run!" He repeats the command.

Like a secretary bird chasing a snake in tall grass, I turn around and on wobbly legs run to where I'm commanded to run. One. Two. Three steps. I turn to see and hear his approval of how I am carrying out his command. But to my shock, he is looking with one eye closed, through the rifle sights to take a good aim at the back of my head. A cold shiver races through my body, my mouth feels as dry as a desert. I continue to look at him in the eyes, yes, the way my father had told me to look at a vicious dog that is about to attack me. The darkness that I saw in the barrel of that rifle is still etched in my mind until today. After this battle of looks he lowers the rifle and goes to sit down where he had removed himself a few minutes earlier. Those few minutes are as long as a lifetime to me. Within that lifetime I have died and risen. I realised later that when death looks into a person's eyes one has to accept it at that moment. Many questions invaded my mind, but this one topped the list: what would have happened if I had not turned to look? Would he have fired and killed me, an unarmed person? Later when I told my cellmate at the police camp about this, he told me that soldier had come up with a way of killing people by accusing them of wanting to run away.

It is when I come to sit down next to Jane's boyfriend that my body begins to shake from the realisation of what could have happened. I imagine myself dead lying there and these soldiers continuing with their lives as if nothing has happened – the way people behave after the killing of snake. Maybe they would talk about how I fell and kicked my legs as my life seeped out of my body. Sweat starts to pour down my body and I'm not sure if it is because of hunger or the fear that had invaded my body when I looked into the barrel of that rifle.

Jane's boyfriend does not want to look at me anymore. He is avoiding my eyes the way children avoid looking at their naked parents taking a bath by the side of the bridge they are crossing – pretending as if they have not seen them. I wonder what is going through his mind; is he thinking about the innocence of what we had been talking about before the other soldier wanted to trick me into dying from his bullet? Is he thinking of what may have happened to me had I not turned to wage an ogling battle with his colleague?

The shadows are short. We almost walk on top of them when the soldiers pack up: small gas stoves, mess cans, ration boxes, cigarette packs – all disappear into their knapsacks. They throw the bags onto their backs after strapping their bullet webbings around their waists. The one who wanted to shoot me fires a few tracer bullets into the grass thatch of the huts under which we have been sitting and they catch fire. Fresh smoke goes up into the midday air adding to that which is rising from the smouldering roof beams that have fallen inside the walls of the huts that have been set on fire before they took their break for breakfast.

We leave the village in single file. From the direction we are taking – east – I am sure that we are bound for the small town which acted as the security forces' base. The soldiers, the police, auxiliary soldiers and the SB all have their offices in this small establishment. Some villagers have relocated to the establishment for fear of being in the crossfire whenever there is a battle in the villages. Others have come for protection since they had been sell-outs and knew that they will be in trouble if the freedom fighters caught up with them. This is where we are headed. It is quite some distance – at least fifteen kilometres if my estimation is right. From where we have been camped for breakfast, we can see some of the buildings that make up the small town.

There are many soldiers in this troop – about thirty – so much that the file is as long as three hundred metres considering that they are about ten metres in between. This is also the way that the freedom fighters walked when they are moving through the bush; they say it reduces the number of casualties in the event of an ambush. But I cannot be spaced out like the rest of the troop so I am walking in front of Jane's boyfriend. I have to be guarded even though I have my hands handcuffed. The troop commanders are bringing up the rear. The fear of an ambush can be seen by the way how the trekking is organised and carried out. They are checking all the sides as they walk and are always stopping by hand signalling to each other; no smoking is allowed.

As our shadows get longer pointing towards the east, we are also nearing the police camp. Soon we are seeing the whole establishment from across the big river that we must cross to get there. A dip V-shaped valley separates us from the camp. We have to walk along the road that connects the police camp to the villages to the west. People are hurrying towards those villages like ants just before a big storm because of the six-to-six curfew that had been put to limit the movement of people at night. As we pass them, they look at me and quickly look away. I must be a spectre walking with the living.

Confusion mixed with fear resides in my mind now. What is going to happen to me? That alone is the question that troubles my mind. I am worried. I am worried about my parents especially my mother. Although we are eight children, one thing that I knew and with pride is that she loved me very much. She loved me because I had proved to be the brightest of her children. Although she herself had gone to school up to Standard 1 she wanted us, her children, to have an education. She often said that I had a soft head, a head that was capable of absorbing school work with ease. She had her own unorthodox way of determining my intelligence. The fact that I enjoyed eating raw groundnuts, and I could remember English words with ease made her conclude that I was clever and, indeed, in my family and in my clan, I was the first to attain an O level education. For twenty-four hours now, she has not heard about where I was. Worry must be killing her; she may not be eating anything. The only person who knew what had happened to me was the owner of the garden in which I had been found. My hope is that he will send word to my mother.

Now that we are in the neighbourhood of the police basecamp; the soldiers have abandoned the file formation that they were using when we were walking in the bush, along the cattle trails. They are walking in groups; there is no fear of being ambushed anymore; they are even smoking and some even speak on top of their voices; they are happy to be back without having lost any one of them. I've heard them say that there will be lots of celebrations that evening – drinking and dancing.

"Tichaona." I stop and turn around to look at the man who has called me. "Stop there."

It is Jane's boyfriend.

"Here, go back home." He has a key in his hand and with it he removes the handcuffs from my wrists. From his camouflage jacket he takes out a pack of cigarettes and pulls out three before giving the rest to me.

Without much fawning, I start off towards where I had come from. Since it is almost six o'clock and the curfew is just about to come into effect, I walk quickly, passing the other soldiers who have been behind us. I'm thinking that the moment I cross the river I must get into the bush, maybe sleep there until tomorrow morning or walk through the dark on my way home. My mind is also running along the trail which we have been walking along to get here, following it like a fire that follows a trail of petrol on the ground. The smell of my mother's cooking, the comfort of my

130

blankets, the coolness of the water at the river where we do our bathing, were all inviting me home. I curse the war; I curse the white settlers; I curse the freedom fighters; I curse everyone who has something to do with the war around me.

By now I'm approaching the bridge across the river and I can see that soldier who wanted to shoot me earlier on walking with two others who probably were his next in command. My stomach muscles tighten and my mouth goes dry as if a fire has been lit in there – the kind of dryness I had experienced when he wanted to shoot me. They are deep in conversation as I pass them without looking at them. When I had gone two steps behind them the man calls me to stop and come back.

"Where are you going now?"

"Your colleagues have told me to go back home."

"I'm the leader of this troop. You're not going anywhere unless I say so. There run to them. They know what to do with you."

My legs are weak, my heart is depressed as I'm shooed to the police camp like a lost ox is driven towards the kraal where it doesn't belong. When at the police camp, I'm unceremoniously re-handcuffed and escorted by two armed policemen to the holding cells. I'm literally thrown inside and before I could stand up from where I had fallen the heavy iron door clangs shut with a finality that echoes in my ears for a long time.

# Chapter 14: Those Shadows on the Wall

We are sitting in the heat of Grandmother's round kitchen hut. Mother is making *sadza* on the fireplace which is at the centre of the hut. My brother, who is two years my senior, sits on the earthen bench which is built along one side of the round hut, the side opposite where the door swings when opened. We are the only children there. I am sitting beside Mother, near the fire. I have to brave and dodge the porridge jumping out of the boiling pot. The sun has set about an hour ago and therefore the paraffin lamp has been lit and sits on the huva, a mound-like bench built furthest from the door of the hut where Grandmother's clay pots are stacked majestically, the biggest at the bottom and the smallest at the top. There are two such sets of these beautifully decorated pots. These are the pride of every housewife in any village.

The yellow light of the paraffin lamp is flickering casting our grotesque shadows on the soil plastered walls behind us, each according to the angle that they face the flickering lamp. The air in the hut smells of burnt maize meal which is falling into the fire as Mother wrestles the big black pot with the thickening contents, her knee anchoring it by the long black handle lest it moves off the fireplace with her vigorous arm swings. From outside, the cry of a nightjar filters to our ears whenever a spell of silence is found in-between commands from Mother or Grandmother: fetch some more firewood; bring down the plates; bring the lamp closer for me to see what I am doing; put your hand on your mouth when you cough. Such was the day to day routine that our lives followed at this time of the day.

In a little while Mother is done with the pot of *sadza*. She has covered it with the lid to allow it to simmer before she removes it from the fire. Now again it goes pfu-u, pfu-u as heated air escapes from inside. She asks my brother to bring down the plates in which she is going to dish the hot, white steaming *sadza*. My brother brings down the plates from the wooden shelf hanging and on the left side of the huva, but in his haste, one of the plates slips small hands. It crushes on the floor. The enamel paint chips off. I could hear it as it continues crackling as it detaches itself from the plate.

"Break them all! When your father comes out of prison he will buy them for me." Grandmother curses my brother. Her voice cracks like thunder in the dimly lit hut. A rat runs along the wall between the roof and the wall. It is as if it has been startled by the old lady's voice.

When the plates are positioned on the dung smeared floor, Mother cuts pieces of *sadza* and puts them in them. The plates in Grandmother's kitchen hut are assigned to all those who eat there.

So, Mother is careful to reduce the size of *sadza* when dishing into our plates. Grandmother's eyes are moving with the dishing spatula.

"Mother-in-law, dishing *sadza* is done." Mother announces as if Grandmother is not in the same hut with all of us.

Grandmother sidles closer to the fireplace and begins to share the chicken. We all know Mother is not allowed to share chicken. If it was okra or *mufushwa* of dried pumpkin leaves, Grandmother did not care. Mother could share that and she would not even bother to announce having finished dishing *sadza*.

"Bring that light closer for me, you." She pokes my brother with her long bony forefinger.

133

Grandmother begins by putting soup into each plate after which she puts the feet of the chicken into my brother's plate and mine – one each. We are all anxiously watching what she is doing. In Mother's plate she throws a wing and a gizzard. The rest goes into her plate such that there are more chicken cuts than the *sadza*.

I can see that Mother is not happy at all. Since we came to stay with Grandmother after Father was arrested she had often said she wished she had her own hut but her mother-in-law did not grant her that wish. She wanted someone to do the house chores for her and Mother had come at the right time for that. Lately she has started to complain of a backache that Mother often suspected was not there at all.

We start eating. As usual when it is *sadza* with chicken we skirt around the chicken feet for if the soup takes us. My brother and I are playing a who-will-finish-his-chicken-foot- first game. Whoever finishes last will then taunt the other by eating as if the other had not been given his share. Young as we are life presents fun all the time. I am only four and my brother is six. We had our freedoms when we were staying at our home. As young as we were we had not been introduced much to table manners. We chew with our mouths open and make a lot of noise as we chew and this did not go down well with Grandmother. We licked our fingers as we ate. Since we came to stay with her, and we have been staying with her for about two weeks now, she has always been accusing Mother of not teaching us good manners. So, as we eat and play all those games, Grandmother looks at us with that eye that says: uncultured brats, one day I will get you. We are not concerned with her speaking eyes. It is when I hiccup with food in my mouth that the storm breaks out.

"*Muroora*, your children are full." She jumps up despite her daily complains of backache and pulls the plates from us. She throws our

134

food to the dogs that happily wag their tails by the door only to leave us licking our fingers. Mother looks away. Wells of tears are flooding her eyes but these cannot be seen on her grotesque shadow dancing on the wall.

# Chapter 15: The Class

The day is done. It's twelve o'clock according to the cannon that just boomed at The Castle. Our day in this classroom is very short because we don't want to keep the street kids for long in a supervised environment. We have been advised by a City of Cape Town psychologist that these children needed their free time so that they can go back to the street and carry on with their kind of life. We shouldn't restrict them within the four walls.

Zuko goes to switch off the Vimvacs that have been busy picking after the kids. The whole classroom floor has been strewn with tins of paint, brushes of all kinds and sizes and pieces of cartridge paper that they have been working with this morning. It has been very windy outside today and therefore we decided to do our painting indoors and on smaller surfaces. The hope is that tomorrow it will be calm and we will go back to painting the walls of the city buildings again.

There are only eight kids today. Most of them have gone to Sea Point where a certain health-related NGO has, throughout the week, been inviting street kids for immunisation against HIV. The ones we have in class have already attended the immunisation course. It is free for them, but for people like us one has to part with a couple of hundreds of rand.

Our classroom is one of a kind. Its walls are actually four flat TV screens which have been pushed right up to the side walls of the room where they meet another flat screen – the ceiling. It is on these screens that we do our illustrations with the electronic brushes that are on a rack which is on the only small table in the middle of the room. We have no chairs or tables for the learners.

Furniture tends to formalise things, ours is an informal learning environment. Our learners sit on the floor which is generously carpeted. The kids copy the illustrations onto cartridge paper using the usual brushes that are standing in tins near the easels. It is amazing how these kids can use these brushes to create paintings of the quality that we have copied and uploaded onto the back flat screen which we use for displays only. There are paintings of wild life, landscapes, skyscapes, cityscapes, portraits of other learners and abstracts on display. I have no doubt that if one of the paintings were to go on the market they would fetch enough money to sustain the life of a street kid throughout a year.

'Okay, boys and girls. The session is over. Let's meet again tomorrow at the same time.' Zuko shouts at the top of his voice in order to be heard. It is incredible how only a few kids could make such a commotion – a busy commotion! The eight kids – three girls and five boys – are excited about their achievements the way two young parents are excited about their first-born child.

'But we've not discussed what we've done like we always do when we paint murals on the city walls!' One of the cute little girls comes to me begging. She is a white girl of about fourteen.

'That means another hour and a half inside this place. You know every one of us has something to say about every painting so far done. Why can't we …?' I'm cut short by the boy standing close to Zuko. He is Coloured with dark wild hair that is almost turning into dreadlocks.

'It's our time and these are creations of our own. Remember there is no hurry in Africa.' We all laugh at this cliché which has survived over eight decades of use on the continent. Some of the kids give each other high fives.

'Well, well then. We may as well begin with your painting Aisha.' Zuko cuts in and goes over to the cupboard at the centre of the classroom. He draws out a box from which he takes out ten gogulators and distributes them to each of us. Everyone straps them around their heads covering their faces making their eyes appear bigger behind those powerful lenses. Soon the evaluation session begins.

Aisha is a Coloured girl of about thirteen. She says that her mother and father had separated and gone different ways one winter morning, leaving her alone under the bridge between Langa and Bonteheuwel train stations. That place had been their home since time immemorial to Aisha. She had then drifted to Cape Town CBD to join the *others* there, not because she was looking for company, but because she had heard that there was a place in the CBD where one could get a plateful of food for the price of a copper five-cent coin that she could easily pick up on the pavement at the train station or at the Golden Arrow bus terminus. She is a very intelligent and precocious.

Aisha's painting is that of the grotesquery genre. Observing it through the gogulators makes it even more bizarre and grotesque but clearer. In it you see a woman's figure. The top part of the woman is thin while the bottom is wide with very large protruding buttocks while the legs tapper out towards the toes. It is so simply done that a casual look at it will relegate it to the trash can, but with the gogulators on, one will be able to see the intricacies in it easily and accurately. It represents the feminine structure of the woman of the South. The gogulators are good when it comes to looking at abstract paintings. They make one see the passion in the strokes of the paint brush, the elegance on the contours and curves presented and can actually give an evaluation that can be converted to monetary value. I recently acquired them from Zimbabwe where they have been used in the stone sculpture evaluation. We use them mainly when we discuss the murals that we would have painted on the city buildings. They are an African invention which has spread to Europe and America and even Japan despite the loud hullabaloo about the inferiority quality placed on things coming out of Africa.

'What is the theme of your painting, Aisha?' Zuko asks as he adjusts his gogulators.

'African feminism.'

'Wow! I didn't expect that from you.' I'm impressed. I can see Zuko is also surprised by this show of knowledge. We look at each other like two parents found in a compromising position by their three-year-old daughter. We have been with these kids for a month and half only.

'In other words, you're celebrating the African female body shape, aren't you?' I ask the girl.

'Oh, yes.' She says confidently. 'The African female body shape is very distinct, so elegant, so lithe, so unique, so luxurious and so unlike that of women from the West or any other part of the world. I've had to use smooth brush strokes especially around the bum and bust to accentuate this. Such paintings are not new. They've been put on canvas since the times of Leonardo da Vinci. But then it was the men who were doing it. Mine is informed by our very own Sarah Baartman.' Aisha adjusts her gogulators and brings them to the price evaluation point. Everybody else follows suit.

'This is a remarkable painting, Aisha. Now, can anyone tell us from their gogulators' point view how much this painting can fetch on the market?' I ask the kids although my gogulators are already bleeping and flashing the monetary value as I look at the painting.

'My gogulators say if it was on canvas it can fetch anything above nine thousand bucks.' Azola says to everyone's agreement.

'That's a lot of money for a person like you.' Everyone laughs. Azola is a black boy who came from Khayelitsha after his parents had died of AIDS two years ago. He had nowhere to go except to join the street community.

'What's wrong with my personage? You seem to think that I'm cheap to run because I'm a street kid. I may be young but I believe I can do away with nine grand as much as you can. What can you do that I cannot do?' Aisha retorts snarling like an incensed cat.

Freedom of speech! They're never short of it, today's kids. 'Anyway, let's go to the next painting.' I'm saying this to cool down tempers and move on. They can really flare like the solar flares sometimes.

Zowen leads us to his displayed piece of art on the left section of the display flat screen. He is a fifteen-year-old Afrikaaner boy whose life in the streets remains a mystery to all of us because we only see him on the days when we go painting the city walls. We don't know where he sleeps at night. One day he will approach this venue from Woodstock and the next from the harbour. When we registered him, he didn't give us an address like: under the bridge near Arts Cape or Good Hope Centre or in Woodstock Cave or near CTICC as the others did. In our books, it was just Zowen – no surname, no address, no parents - nothing. He was just there and did not want to talk about personal identity.

From a casual glance one is bound to say that Zowen has painted those famous clouds known to appear on Table Mountain once in a while. They are like the fluffy ones created by the katabatic winds flowing down the slopes of the mountain like a table cloth. Clouds? Those are not just clouds hanging there, my gogulators report to my eyes. All of us have to fine tune our gogulators to get a clear scrutiny of the painting. A close gogulator-look reveals that there are pictures and letters imbedded there. When I look at it closer I see the corporate logo of Chase Standard Bank cleverly painted in the clouds. The S carries the C in its lower

140

curve and the B is in the upper curvature, all this contained in a circle that is blurred by the light strokes of the brush. What looks like the blue sky and the white of the clouds are the corporate colours of the bank. I'm sure if this is going to be shown to the CEO of the bank they are likely going to adopt it. It is a masterpiece that requires clever eyes to decipher the import of its message. It is easy to see all this through the gogulators. CSB is the bank that is sponsoring the classroom and what is inside it. It also pays us handsomely for running this project.

'What is the theme of your piece?' I ask Zowen.

'This is abstract art like you always say when a piece of art looks like mine there. That's all I can say. I've no idea what a theme is. This picture must speak for itself. I think that's the thing about art. The seer must say what they see. I'm not here to tell art lovers what to see in my work. What I'm trying to say, however, is: thank you CSB for giving us a chance to do something worthwhile with our lives. I must tell you I've never been in a classroom. I learnt how to read and write my name informally. This is my first time to have some people control what I do, when I do it and how I do it.'

We all look at Zowen. He is looking at the floor like a small child caught playing with his boyhood by her mother. He seems to be saying: I've said what I mustn't have said. We did not know this little information about Zowen. It poses a challenge to all of us, that is, Zuko and me. Most of the street kids we have in our class are school drop-outs due to one reason or another – death of parents due to HIV and AIDS, abandonment when mothers get married by other men, etc. For instance, Aisha dropped out of school because her parents decided to separate. Although the family was living under the bridge, the girl had attended Mimosa Primary School in Bonteheuwel for seven years. I can see that Zuko is also unprepared for what Zowen had said.

'I'm sorry to hear that, Zowen. Come everyone, we'll finish this evaluation tomorrow. The day is done. You must be hungry too. Remove your gogulators and place them carefully in that box. Let's meet here same time tomorrow if it's windy. If it's not, we meet at the CTICC. We need to finish the murals on the N1 side of the conference centre. Ok?'

There's disappointment on the faces of those whose work has not been appraised. As they file out, some of them light up stubs of cigarettes they had extinguished when they came in. I can even pick the whiff of *ganja*. Our classroom is a smoke free zone. This we have stamped into their minds on the very first day that they walked in. We make sure this is observed without question. The rule riles Zuko as much as the kids, but that was a rule to be followed like a train on steel rails. Although I smoke too, I obey this rule religiously.

'What do you think of this?' I ask Zuko as I switch on the Vimvacs for a final run on the thick carpet of our classroom.

'Think of what, Tendeka? I don't understand.' The two of us stand there watching the machines run around gobbling any small objects on the floor. The machines are very thorough. Zuko switches off the flat screens surrounding us.

'You mean you fail to see what I'm saying. Freedom brought a lot of changes in this country. A white child growing up illiterate was unheard of during apartheid.'

'*Bhuti*, gone are those days when whites used to hide their inadequacies and failures. This is real South Africa in Africa forty-five years after gaining freedom. Know what, my step-grandfather told me that the white people used to hide their daughters who would have fallen pregnant outside marriage. The babies from such circumstances were put up for adoption immediately after birth and sometimes the mothers were declared mad. That's how they hid

142

issues like teenage pregnancies that were never part of the national statistics.'

'Oh, yes. I've heard about that. They even used to give each other jobs, loans to cover the fact that some of them were as poor as people of colour in this country. Look, today we give them R2 at the traffic lights just like what we do to the blacks and the coloureds. So,' Zuko looks at me before saying, 'what do you suggest we must do about Zowen?'

'I was thinking about that too. Our class should not only be for aesthetics but I think we need also to introduce academics to help street kids like Zowen. We need to introduce the teaching of reading and writing to those kids in Zowen's predicament. This is 2039. We can't have kids who cannot read and write.'

The following day, we've a full complement of our register – ten boys and seven girls. A simple survey reveals to us that out of all of these kids seven have never seen the inside of a classroom for the purpose of learning the ABCs of reading and writing. So, we group the class according to this finding. We approach CSB. CSB hears our story and donates seven compubets. I start teaching the kids how to read and write while Zuko looks after those who are free ranging. What I instruct them to do with the compubets is to say a sound into the microphone of the machine and see how it is written on the small compubet screen. The learner can also punch in a syllable and the compubet says the sound out for him or her to repeat. This I find out is the easiest way to teach these kids. It takes away most of the teacher talk and gives the learners an opportunity to teach themselves. This is a Ugandan invention that was patented during Museveni's dictatorship so that people can teach their children reading and writing privately in their homes. During that time Ugandans feared the brainwashing methods of instruction that had been introduced in schools.

With these gadgets, there is much room for experimentation. It is difficult for the learners at first but after sometime of playing around with the gizmos the seven street kids gain confidence. At the end of the first lesson they are able to write some syllables and mouth them with ease. They are also able to write their names and to identify their written forms. For Zowen it is an experience that he had missed and it seems to breathe a new life into him.

Of course, we have disciplinary problems here and there, now and again. The commonest form of indiscipline comes from those kids who come after having sniffed glue or smoked *ganja*. They are sometimes so unruly and cannot conform to simple set rules; therefore, we've to put in place mechanisms to check such behaviour. For instance, the door into our classroom is opened by breathing into a breathalyser and if anyone is high on any drug or liquor the door doesn't open for them. It is such an effective deterrent that our indiscipline problems are reduced to almost nil.

There are also wrist bands called compubands that every kid has to put on both wrists when they enter the classroom. These have been designed in Zimbabwe for those people who were opposing the Mugabe government after the disputed 2023 elections which saw many opposition party supporters being thrown into prison for dissent. There, these gadgets had proved very useful at Chikurubi Maximum Prison. They can render anyone who wants to beat another person weak in the elbows and wrists. All these machines are controlled by monitors which are incorporated in the flat screens.

Our class follows no time table except for the non-readers and non-writers, even these ones we sometimes let them work on their own to improve on whatever area they wish in their reading and writing. Each learner gets to choose what they want to do for the day except when we go painting the city walls. They work on their chosen projects until they are sure they have mastered and perfected it. As always, we set the last hour of the day for the evaluation of the day's art pieces. Thus, we provide a learning environment which allows our learners to freely explore their minds' creativity.

Within a year, our class is hitting the educational headlines and requests for tours and visits start pouring in from principals in the Western Cape. We appear on national television; our pictures are in newspapers and magazines with us standing around while the kids are lying down on the carpeted floor busy with their gizmos. Stories and documentaries of how we have managed to transform the classroom into a free learning zone have gone viral world-wide. We are invited to talk-shows together with our learners where we are asked about our inner-city project. Zuko has been telling me a municipality in the USA has sent him an email inviting us there to help them set up such classes. Who knew we could be celebrities when we started this project?

Printed in the United States
By Bookmasters